Son *was*

Cynth~~ia~~ ~~I believe you're~~ ~~going.~~ Tyler considered opening his eyes, but he'd decided he was dreaming, and he didn't want to quit the dream. Not yet.

"Tyler," whispered the dream. The dream had a low, sexy voice that tickled his ear. Tyler stayed still, his eyes firmly closed.

"We have a room, love. A very quiet room. It's so much more comfortable than this booth. So much more private than this booth. Wouldn't you like that? I would like that, Tyler. I want to see you, I want to feel you. I want to taste you."

One eye opened, because when tasting was involved, reality was always better than dreams.

Oh, Edie.

Blaze

Dear Reader,

Eight years ago we moved from Texas to New York, and it was an eye-opening experience. There are two separate cultures, both with their positives and negatives, and for many years, I would simply people-watch, listen and crack myself up.

I have always enjoyed hearing people's stories, and my friends and the anonymous checker in the grocery store have no idea how much these little bits of their life inspire me.

Family secrets are a staple of drama, but recently, I've seen how real-life secrets, how the sudden realization that life isn't always what you think it is, can turn a family inside out. And thus, *Just Surrender...* was born.

I hope you enjoy visiting with the Hart family. They're a little wounded, but very, very loveable.

All the best,

Kathleen O'Reilly

Kathleen O'Reilly

JUST SURRENDER...

TORONTO NEW YORK LONDON
AMSTERDAM PARIS SYDNEY HAMBURG
STOCKHOLM ATHENS TOKYO MILAN MADRID
PRAGUE WARSAW BUDAPEST AUCKLAND

If you purchased this book without a cover you should be aware
that this book is stolen property. It was reported as "unsold and
destroyed" to the publisher, and neither the author nor the
publisher has received any payment for this "stripped book."

Recycling programs
for this product may
not exist in your area.

ISBN-13: 978-0-373-79615-1

JUST SURRENDER...

Copyright © 2011 by Kathleen Panov

All rights reserved. Except for use in any review, the reproduction or
utilization of this work in whole or in part in any form by any electronic,
mechanical or other means, now known or hereafter invented, including
xerography, photocopying and recording, or in any information storage
or retrieval system, is forbidden without the written permission of the
publisher, Harlequin Enterprises Limited, 225 Duncan Mill Road,
Don Mills, Ontario, Canada M3B 3K9.

This is a work of fiction. Names, characters, places and incidents are
either the product of the author's imagination or are used fictitiously,
and any resemblance to actual persons, living or dead, business
establishments, events or locales is entirely coincidental.

This edition published by arrangement with Harlequin Books S.A.

For questions and comments about the quality of this book
please contact us at Customer_eCare@Harlequin.ca.

® and TM are trademarks of the publisher. Trademarks indicated with
® are registered in the United States Patent and Trademark Office, the
Canadian Trade Marks Office and in other countries.

www.Harlequin.com

Printed in U.S.A.

ABOUT THE AUTHOR

Kathleen O'Reilly wrote her first romance at the age of eleven, which to her undying embarrassment was read aloud to her class. After taking more than twenty years to recover from the profound distress, she is now proud to finally announce her career—romance author. Now she is an award-winning author of nearly twenty romances published in countries all over the world. Kathleen lives in New York with her husband and their two children, who outwit her daily.

Books by Kathleen O'Reilly

HARLEQUIN BLAZE
297—BEYOND BREATHLESS*
309—BEYOND DARING*
321—BEYOND SEDUCTION*
382—SHAKEN AND STIRRED**
388—SEX, STRAIGHT UP**
394—NIGHTCAP**
485—HOT UNDER PRESSURE†
515—MIDNIGHT RESOLUTIONS†
541—LONG SUMMER NIGHTS†

*The Red Choo Diaries
**Those Sexy O'Sullivans
†Where You Least Expect It

To get the inside scoop on Harlequin Blaze and its talented writers, be sure to check out blazeauthors.com.

Don't miss any of our special offers. Write to us at the following address for information on our newest releases.

Harlequin Reader Service
U.S.: 3010 Walden Ave., P.O. Box 1325, Buffalo, NY 14269
Canadian: P.O. Box 609, Fort Erie, Ont. L2A 5X3

To Kathryn Lye.

We writers get obsessively attached to our words.
So often I hear other authors complain about
the editors who make their words worse.
Thank you to the one who makes mine better.

1

EDIE HIGGINS DRUMMED her black-polished nails happily as she sat behind the wheel of Barnaby's cab. The midnight rain flowed down the windshield in rivers, her Mickey Mouse watch said 1:07 a.m., but JFK airport was still bustling with life. The May air was warm, but not too warm, which was a good thing, because Edie had quickly discovered that the A/C in Barnaby's cab had gone out since the last time she'd driven it. Not that the brakes were in great condition either, but it so happened that Edie had a lead foot, which worked just as well for stopping as speeding up.

Curious, she scanned the soggy travelers that were waiting in the long taxi line. Since she had been a kid, she had always adored the drama of airports. The heart-squeezing hugs of families coming home, the long, wet kisses of reunited lovers and the misty-eyed wave from a forlorn six-year-old who didn't understand why Mom was going away. That was life. The connections people craved. That was what made Edie sigh.

By her own rudimentary calculations, this late on a Thursday should be the pièce de résistance: tourist night. A boredom-busting extravaganza during which she could drive dewy-eyed couples to their getaway destinations. Or whisk away families to the overpriced tourist trap that was the Great White Way.

Hey, whatever made them happy. And that was the part she liked most. Watching people as they bubbled with anticipation, their faces glowing from that champagne-like awareness. The knowledge that good things were about to happen.

Now *that* made her sigh.

She grabbed her phone and checked her voice mail, just in case he had called.

"You have no messages," the voice answered, and Edie stuffed the phone in her bag. No reason to think about missing phone calls, about people who didn't need her, when there were thousands of people desperate to get out of the rain, which was exactly the reason she was here.

Slowly she inched the cab forward. The water-soaked attendant was shoving passengers into yellow cabs like yesterday's garbage. Beneath the flickering security lights, Edie perused the cab line, counting heads to discover her prize. The gnarly attendant, not on board with the whole "customer service" concept, ripped open the back door. Edie shot a look over her shoulder, anticipating what exciting adventure the passenger lottery had shelled out tonight.

Would it be canoodling lovers, or shrieking families? No. Instead, it was Mr. Overly Practical, No-Champagne-for-Me Trench Coat, who clearly wouldn't know adventure unless he looked it up in the dictionary. He wore a dark suit and a striped tie secured in a perfect Windsor knot, which she knew only because her dad—the esteemed Dr. Jordan Higgins, M.D.—loved the Windsor knot. It was crisp, professional and reeked of glory.

Just. Like. Dr. Jordan Higgins.

As with so many things that the esteemed Dr. Jordan Higgins loved, Edie despised the Windsor knot.

Not to be overly critical, but okay, she hated the striped ties, too. They were an oxygen-stifling invention, similar to women's hose, meant to entrap humanity in a constricting uniform of sameness. Taking a sneak peek in the rearview mirror, she noted the man's impeccable reflection that defied travel wrinkles…or any semblance of life.

Great. She'd given up free drinks with Anita to drive the cab, and yes, Barnaby could always twist her arm—not hard because of her must-be-recessive sucker-gene—but still…

At least his hair was mussed, she thought as he settled his briefcase neatly next to him on the seat. The rain had darkened his rampant locks black with one woebegone strand hanging damply into his eyes. Impatiently he pushed at it, restoring it to its normal spot.

It was a pity because he was so much more appealing when he was mussed. But hey, not everyone could identify and exploit their intrinsic advantages like Edie could. Not that she would say a word. Trench coats never took criticism well, so she pulled onto the Belt Parkway, aka Pothole Crater of America, and eased into the slow-moving traffic. "Where to, mister?"

"The Belvedere Hotel," he answered, which startled her only because the Belvedere was more than a little naughty, completely not a Windsor knot type place—unless the ties were the kinky silk and satin kind. Edie scrutinized her passenger with new, more appreciative eyes. *Kink?*

"Seriously?"

"Just drive," he instructed, his voice crisply impersonal, accustomed to being obeyed. Edie, never a lapdog, tapped her fingers on the wheel.

"Meeting somebody at the hotel?" she asked.

Cooly he met her eyes in the mirror, then glanced at the
ID tag on the visor. "You don't look like Barnaby."

"The marvel of medical science. Two years of hormones,
a few surgeries and voilà, Barbara."

"Not likely," he muttered, choosing to spoil her fun with
his nay-saying truth. When she glanced in the mirror again,
that lock of hair had stubbornly fallen back into his eyes.
Edie smiled. Sometimes there was a God, and sometimes
She had a sense of humor.

"Barnaby's my ex," she admitted.

"Your ex lets you drive his cab? That has to be ille-
gal."

Edie shrugged. To her the law was another constricting
set of mandates, much like the Windsor knot. "His Uncle
Marty is some hoo-haw at the taxi and limousine commis-
sion. I don't think they're actually related—it's an implied
relationship, informal and forged through extensive bribes.
Barnaby gets away with more than most."

"What's your real job?"

"Real job?" Edie scoffed. "What is that, exactly? Some
greed-inspired drudgery that people consider socially acceptable. Eight hours of vomitus detail, mind-eroding
minutia and arguments over possibly purloined office
supplies. No thank you. However, in the interest of full
disclosure and because I don't want to get Uncle Marty
in trouble, I don't drive the cab very often. Mainly when
Barnaby sets up a date with Sasha, which usually falls on
Thursdays when he's supposed to have class—not that he'll
be at school, because he dropped out last semester."

"Why all the secrecy?" he asked, and immediately
Edie knew that he had never had an overbearing, interfer-
ing family. Not that she had one, either. But she'd always
longed for one—something big with lots of loud brothers
and sisters, like the ones on sitcoms.

As she cruised through the toll booths, she decided to

let him in on the ins and outs of the American Family Dynamic. "They keep the relationship in the closet because Barnaby's family doesn't approve. She's from Oklahoma, and his parents are really uptight about the whole situation because they have this weird anti-Oklahoma thing, so sometimes he calls me up, and I drive the cab. Usually on a Thursday, which I like because it's a good night for a people person like myself."

With a sharp veer to the left, she shot in front of a cabbie who hadn't learned the ropes, and then swore as the traffic ground to a full stop. Tonight the Belt was packed with cars, red brake lights glowing eerily through the rain. Somewhere up ahead, there was the unfulfilled promise of road construction.

Given the pouring rain, it followed that there would be no crews on the job. Which left only the department of transportation-mandated lane closures. There was a screwy logic to New York, you just had to embrace it. Mr. Trench Coat wasn't the embraceable type.

Seeing an opening two lanes over, she sped up before slamming on the brakes, and then tried not to smile when Mr. Trench Coat hit his head.

Edie believed there was a certain responsibility in playing the part of a New York cabbie. There were expected rude behaviors and bad-driving norms. Frankly, it was all fiction—well, not all—but Edie chose to give people their money's worth.

"You don't care that your ex is seeing someone new?" he asked, completely calm.

"We didn't click," she explained as she creatively maneuvered the traffic, but not once did he blink, swear or wipe sweat from his brow. Damn it.

After jamming down on the horn at one excruciatingly slow Jersey driver, she grinned and then cursed the entire garden state to various transportation woes including rate hikes, speeding ticket quotas and exploding water mains, with liquid glowing green.

A quick glance over her shoulder confirmed that her passenger was ignoring her driving, which disappointed her and made her wonder if she was losing her touch. Nothing that couldn't be fixed.

"I tried to make it work," Edie continued, dodging to hit every road crater that she could. "The sex was pretty good, but Barnaby never knew what to talk about, no imagination. Not a romantic bone in his—frankly, a little on the skinny-side—body. I have to tell ya, it got boring fast. Never a good sign in a relationship. Besides, a woman can tell. Within five minutes I know if a guy is the one."

"Five minutes? That long?" She heard the disbelief in his voice, but she had been confronted by doubters before, and Edie loved to argue. There were universal truths in the world, especially when it came to romance, and the more men that were educated in said truths, the better for womenkind everywhere.

"Oh, sure, pretend you don't do the same thing. Science has proven that people know pretty much instantly. I prefer not to waste my time. Life's too short to ignore what's in front of your nose. Or what's not." Much of what she said was complete nonsense, but the last part was true.

"And what are these signs that a person is supposed to be looking for to recognize the *one?*"

He was mocking her, making fun of what he thought was foolish, silly and possibly naive. She hated that her shoulders immediately tensed, but she had been branded the fool before—by people whose opinion mattered—and it didn't bother her. Much.

"You can think whatever you want, but as for me, I'm looking for lightning. Thunder. AC/DC playing in my head. The world has to tilt and shift—and I have to forget how to breathe."

"That's not love, that's stress cardiomyopathy."

She knew that man-tone, that Sahara-dry voice, dismissing anything that couldn't be proven through the scientific method. As if love could be proven or disproven. It simply was. "Wiseass, aren't you?"

Obviously accustomed to the insult, he chose to ignore it. "How often have you experienced these symptoms?"

"Never."

"You're setting yourself up for failure," he pronounced, a blow to Hallmark, romance and the entire speed-dating industry.

"Life is full of failures. If you don't fail, you've failed to truly live. I'll take my chances."

It should have made her happy that he didn't argue further, but it didn't. Dr. Jordan Higgins never argued, either. No matter how outrageous, no matter how controversial. Edie cranked up the radio, but the volume wasn't working, and it wasn't loud enough to drown out the silence, so Edie switched it off.

Eventually, she broke down and turned to classic dinner-party conversation. "You're Cancer, aren't you?" she asked.

"Not the last time I checked."

"Your sign. Cancer. Reticent, inflexible, deep thinker."

"Gemini."

Dazzling wit? Impulsive? "No way."

"Yes way," he insisted.

Unable to reconcile this astrological anomaly, she abandoned personal conversation until they hit the BQE. As they zoomed along, she pointed out the various tourist sites flying by, but her "Welcome to New York" spiel was interrupted by a beep.

Mr. Trench Coat had a text message.

She stopped talking, easily imagining the words on his phone. For his sake, she hoped it was something sexy, possibly visual, suggestive, earthy, but not tacky. *Subtle* went a long way in seduction. Edie considered herself something of an expert at the art of love.

After a second he swore, euphemistically alluding to the carnal arts, but not in a sexy way. He sounded pissed.

When she checked his expression, she noticed the way the brows furrowed into the broad forehead. The hair was still in his eyes.

The dude was screwed.

"Something wrong?" she asked, trying to sound innocent rather than nosy.

"Nothing."

Ha. If that was nothing, then she was a rocket scientist. Not that she couldn't be if she wanted. Edie had aced two courses in astrophysics at NYU, but had changed majors after a heated discussion with the prof on the viability of red giants, white dwarfs and the antifeminist fairy-tale ideology that perpetuates the idea that one woman should be subjected to the sexual demands of seven professionally challenged men with severe Napoleon complexes.

There were some who thought it was a giant leap of logic to go from stars to anti-feminist literary tropes, including her professor, whom she affectionately called Professor Moriarity. He was not amused, much like her silent passenger, who was staring blindly out the window. She felt a quiver of sympathy, which caused her to frown, because Windsor knots and trench coats did not deserve sympathy. Of course, they usually didn't swear, either.

"Something's interrupted your plans?" she asked.

"The only plan I have is to sleep."

Edie laughed, and then exited toward the Whitestone Bridge. "At the Belvedere? Not that your accommodations are any of my business, but I'm dying to know, so if you want to volunteer the details, I'm a very captive audience."

He looked away from the window, and met her eyes in the mirror. Perfectly arched brows furrowed with momentary alarm. About time. "What's with the Belvedere? Is there a problem?"

"You've never stayed there?"

"No. My brother is going to stay there next month, so I though I would try it."

Edie snickered under her breath.

"Damn it."

Poor guy, losing it left and right. Edie didn't want to be nice. First of all, because it would ruin the whole snarling cabbie mystique, but also because trench-coat arrogance was not what she considered a positive trait. And so, yes, for the second time that night, the sucker-gene kicked in. Carefully she picked her words, doing her best not to scare him. "It's not too bad. Different than your typical accommodations. Kind of a couples thing. I knew you didn't look the type, but you know, still waters run deep. And I've been wrong before. Once."

He snickered. She heard it, which made her feel better because laughter, even the scoffing kind, counted for something.

"It doesn't matter. I'm beat. Give me a shot of scotch, clean sheets, a decent surface and I'm out anyway." He ended up with a careless shrug, this from a man who didn't do careless at all.

Edie squinted through the windshield, the rain pelting down, the wipers squeaking. "What are you here for? Business? Pleasure?" she asked, merging to the right to escape the upcoming traffic.

"I was meeting someone." When he answered, his voice was flat, missing both thunder and lightning. In fact, Edie would bet copious amounts of cash that he didn't even know who AC/DC was.

"And thus the Belvedere," she surmised. A romantic

getaway for the romantically challenged. "You should thank your brother for the hotel suggestion when you get back home."

"After I kill him."

This time, she heard the dip in his voice, the Southern drawl so disdained by every self-respecting New Yawker. "Where's home?"

"Houston."

"Sorry."

"Don't be. It's a good city."

"It's not New York," she corrected.

"Have you ever been to Houston?"

"Once. I had an ex who was a bull rider. Leon 'The Ball-Breaker' Braker. I completely bought in to the image until I went to the Houston livestock show. The bull threw him off in two-point-seven seconds, and that was it. I broke up with him the next week. Faker."

"That's very cold of you."

"Nah. I fixed him up with this chick I met in the hotel bar. She was a chiropractor. They're married now."

He resumed the blind stare out the window. He was either directionally challenged or emotionally numb. She was betting on the latter, which made her try even harder to cheer him up.

"This weather's hell. Where's the girlfriend? Flight delayed?"

Instead of cooperating, he stayed silent, choosing not to spill his most private thoughts to a complete stranger.

Since he left her mind to its own creative devices Edie assessed his situation. Girlfriend wasn't showing and he was crushed. Windsor knots never took rejection well, although he didn't seem as heartbroken as she thought he should be. She wondered if he liked quiet redheads because Patience needed to meet a guy who didn't yell. Somebody who knew how to keep his emotions in check, and Mr. Trench Coat was nothing if not repressed.

"She's not showing, is she? Tough beans, but hey, the Belvedere's great for getting to know people. I'll bet you'll meet someone new tonight, a leggy blonde, or maybe twins."

He chose to ignore her attempt to perk him up, which annoyed her, because she was going out of her way to be nice, and why didn't he appreciate it? Most of all, Edie didn't do silence well. Never had.

"Oh, come on. We've got another thirty…fifty…ninety minutes. People bond in long car rides, and I don't like talking to myself. Let's try something easy. Like…how long you two been together?"

"Do we have to talk?" he asked, as the cars behind them started to honk.

"Yes. I'm trying to give you the full New York cabbie experience, so couldn't you try to be a sport? It's an easy question. Just something to keep me going here."

She heard the deep indrawn breath, a slow glacial defrosting sound. "Three years. Or maybe five?"

"You don't know?" she blurted out, not bothering to hide the horror.

"Not exactly. Can we drive now?"

Whoa, boy. No wonder he was getting the cold shoulder. Forget fixing him up with Patience. She deserved better. Gingerly, Edie got the cab moving again. "I can see the problem."

"And I'm sure you have advice."

"No way, buddy. You dug that hole all by yourself. A grave is a dark, damp place late at night."

"If you sleep well, you never know. I always sleep well."

She glanced in the mirror, noted the confidence in his eyes, his face, even the rigid posture, all the while enduring a death-defying motor-vehicle experience. A humiliating moment in Edie's bright cab-driving career that was getting dimmer by the minute.

"I bet you use meds for sleep," she muttered, because she didn't like being a failure at anything. It was a trait inherited from her father—one of the very few that she admitted.

"No meds. You have to be smart about your life. Control stress, eat healthy, exercise."

"Thanks, Mom."

"It's your funeral," he answered.

"Hey, I'm not the one sleeping alone tonight," she shot back. Perhaps it was a petty taunt, but it wasn't like his ego couldn't take it.

"Barnaby?" He sounded shocked. Disapproving.

Delicious.

"Nah," she answered smoothly. "I'll go out trolling after I drop you off. Premeditation takes all the spontaneity out of it. It's like walking around with a lightning rod over your head and pretending to be surprised when the storm hits. What fun is that?"

And he completely bought it. "You're going to go hook up with some stranger?"

"Oh, sure," she gushed, finally discovering which buttons to push. "It's a lot more exciting that way."

"It's unsafe."

"Not if you're smart."

"What if he's a criminal?"

He sounded genuinely concerned. It was sweet, but unnecessary since Edie didn't believe in one-night stands. Sex was part of the biological symbiosis that wove through the earth. You had to follow the strands of karmic DNA that were laid out in front of you, and picking up strange men in clubs was forging a connection that didn't exist.

She noticed his worried frown, and should have eased

up on the man. But not yet. "You can tell a killer by the eyes, cold and flat, missing the soul."

"By that definition, I'm a serial killer."

She smiled. "No, you're not. I can read your eyes."

"Right," he shot back. Cocky, but clueless. Typical. "What do my eyes say?" he asked, possibly because of her dismissing snort.

"You *really* want to know?"

"No."

"Oh, come on, you know you want to."

And once again, he sighed. "Go ahead."

She considered fibbing, but Mr. Trench Coat needed something to perk him up. "You're cold and flat, but you still possess the soul. However, you belong in the Hilton, not the Belvedere."

"Flattering."

"Yet, true," she dared him to deny it.

"Why is Manhattan that way?" he finally asked, his hand pointing to the west. "Shouldn't we be headed in that direction?"

"I thought you'd like to see more of the outer boroughs. Most people don't appreciate the architectural diversity of the city. It's very picturesque."

"I'm not going to pay extra because you got lost."

Lost? Edie? Ha. "Flat rate from the airport to the city. It's the rules."

"Now you're law-abiding?"

"You're just fun to joke with, and you look like you needed cheering up."

"It's late. I'm tired. I want to get to the hotel."

"Are you always this crabby when you're tired?"

"No."

"Don't you want to see Underground New York, the part that tourists always overlook?"

"No."

"At some point, you'll have to get out and see the sights. You can't let rejection get you down. She's not worth it."

"She's not getting me down."

"Oh, yeah, sure. Believe what you want. Tonight, when you're alone in bed staring at that mirror on the ceiling, you'll see those empty eyes. And before I know it, you'll be the front page, having jumped naked from the Brooklyn Bridge."

"A mirror on the ceiling?" he repeated, picking out the least inflammatory bit of her sentence. It said so much about his sexual psyche.

"Of course. You should check out the theater."

"What theater?"

"At the hotel. It's live. The guests can reserve a time slot, and ahem...perform for whoever wants to watch. I heard the seats fill up fast."

"Please, no."

Edie grinned at him in the mirror. "I'm kidding."

"I thought so," he told her, so obviously a lie.

"I'm kidding about the reservations. It's first-come, first-serve."

"I don't believe you," he answered stiffly, but she noticed him pulling at the knot at his throat.

Certainly, some of the Belvedere tales were urban legends, and then some were nothing but Page Six gossip, although Edie firmly believed that where there was smoke, there was usually an arsonist with a can of kerosene and a match that didn't want to light. Frankly, a viewing room sounded fun—as long as the man was sexy, and the woman didn't have leg hair. Edie always shaved. A woman needed some standards.

"Suit yourself."

"Can you just take me to the hotel?" he asked, impatience finally starting to show. Sadly Edie realized that her joyride, such as it was, was over. She'd have to go back to the apartment. Have to listen to her upstairs neighbor and his girlfriend getting hot and sweaty between the sheets. She'd have to stare at bad TV, and listen to the clock ticking in the dark. All of which she hated with a passion.

So okay, perhaps when she took the U-turn in the middle of Nostrand Avenue, it was a little reckless. The car rocked over the curb and Edie jerked at the wheel, pulling tight to the left. At last all four tires were firmly back on the ground. Perhaps a little too firmly because that was when she heard the noise.

For a split second, panic struck her, until she met his gaze in the mirror. Unmoved, and completely in control. Jerk. Quickly, she cleared the anxiety away, and when she spoke, her words sounded almost calming. "What was that?"

His lips curled at the corners, and the cool, emotionless eyes gleamed like the devil. "A flat."

Oh, hell.

2

IT WAS THE NIGHT FROM HELL. If it hadn't been for the raw nerves in the cabbie's expression, he would have been furious, but he'd seen that panic before. In his line of work, he saw the fear of death everyday, and the instinct to take control was second nature to Dr. Tyler Hart M.D.

"Does Barnaby have a spare?" he asked patiently, using his clinical voice.

At his question, she turned to face him, and he could see the shakes receding. Her color was better and the quiver in her eyes was gone. "I don't know."

His mind ran through the steps, making a mental checklist of tools and procedure, and he was happy for the diversion. Changing flats, performing a quadruple bypass—these were the things that he was prepared for. A kiss-off from Cynthia? Not in this lifetime. And Tyler hated being unprepared. "We'll check the trunk."

"Yeah," she agreed, already falling into blind obedience, which peopled tended to do at the sound of his clinical voice. Was it uncertainty, or a sheeplike personality that suddenly made her so agreeable? Considering the magenta streaks in the short blond hair, he was betting on the uncertainty.

The rain pounded on the roof, but regrettably his trench coat would have to go. Tyler wasn't about to sacrifice it to axle grease and New York grime. He took a deep breath, rolled up his sleeves and headed for the great outdoors.

The great outdoors showered his head, and he bit back a curse. Tyler didn't believe in using disrespectful words. It indicated a lack of control, as well as a juvenile vocabulary. Neither of which were necessary because he thrived on bad circumstances. He had pulled off aortal coarctations that were nothing short of miraculous. In the big scheme of things, rain was nothing.

Except a damned inconvenience.

As he waded toward the trunk, he felt her presence behind him. Tyler smiled with relief when he spotted the jack, the lug wrench and the treadless doughnut. Not great, but it'd do.

"Thank God," she whispered in an awed voice. For the first time she didn't sound quite so cavalier. None too soon, either.

It was no surprise when she started to unwedge the tire from the trunk. In fact, he had expected it, but he stopped her with a polite tap on the arm. "I can do this."

"I should do it," she insisted, tugging uselessly on the tire. "I flew over that curb like a rabid bat. And it's my personal dogma that when you do bad, you need to immediately make right, or something worse will come down the pipe."

Something worse? What was she expecting? Famine, pestilence?

Patiently, he met her eyes, watching the rain stream down her face, waiting for wisdom to dawn. Tyler believed that at some point, a person needed to abandon principles and simply do what needed to be done. Her stubborn jawline didn't bode well for foregoing principles, but her irises were getting a little smarter. Eventually, she nodded.

"At least let me help," she suggested—almost sensibly. "If you're going to get soaked and be miserable, I should, too."

Her T-shirt was transparent. Yes, Cynthia had blown off their relationship in a text message—*in a text message*—a fact that really grated, because it seemed rude. Not that he was hurt or disappointed, and he wasn't sure why he wasn't hurt or disappointed, but a text message? Perhaps that was why his macular muscles kept straying to her chest because Tyler wasn't a big fan of carnal philandering. He never had the time nor the inclination, however, the sight of jutting nipples was torpedoing his normal restraint. "Not necessary. Wait in the cab," he instructed.

"Please," she asked, and it was a testament to the power of the sexual dynamic that he stood there, foolishly dripping wet, his gaze locked on her face, which was—unfortunately—nearly as tasty as the twin nipples that he didn't want to want.

Her blond hair was cut short, which he wasn't normally a big fan of, but it worked for her in that "I'm too sexy for a boy" look. His eyes tracked down her chest, then tracked back to the trunk. *The flat.* "Do you have a flashlight? Maybe Barnaby has one in the glove box?"

He didn't need the light, but he didn't want her breasts near him while he worked. The rain, the text message, the punctured tire—everything was starting to flat-line his common sense.

"I don't think Barnaby's that well stocked," she argued, shoving her hands in her jean pockets, which only drew the shirt tighter.

"Can you check? Please?" he pleaded, needing to have her and her tightly packed body out of his sights.

Happily she disappeared, but then returned in a too-short two seconds with a flashlight. Of course. Trying to help, she directed the light beam in the direction of the rear wheel. "I remembered I had one in my bag. It was a giveaway at this Hudson River wildlife and fisheries symposium. It was a few months back, so I'd forgotten."

"Lucky me," he murmured, setting the jack under the axle, and starting to twist off the lug nuts. Twisting tight. Painfully hard. Until he felt something give. Principles. Dogma. Ironlike restraint.

"I'm Edie," she told him, because apparently now was the perfect time for introductions.

Edie. A cute, perky name. With cute, perky breasts. And gamine brown eyes that sparkled in the rain. *Sparkled.* Tyler gave the nut another vicious twist.

"What's your name?" she asked. Her conversation wasn't what he was used to. Tyler liked coldly impersonal, eight-syllable words that didn't involve sex, emotion, or—god-forbid—nipples.

Instead of replying, he pulled even tighter.

"Don't be mad. You know rain is very good for the planet. It's cleansing and nourishing, feeding the parched earth."

"Not in New York," he said, wiping at his face, feeling the moisture cling to his skin. Dirt was unsanitary, a breeding ground for flesh-eating bacteria and flesh-licking sex. Quietly, he groaned.

"I'm sorry," she apologized. Obviously she was finally feeling the guilt that she should have felt several thousand hours ago.

Fully intending to give her a well-deserved lecture, Tyler glanced up, but she looked so…so needy. "I'm Tyler."

"Tyler. Pleased to meet you. You got that?" she asked, just after he finished with the nuts, and was prying off the hubcap.

"Yeah. Doing great," he answered, flinching when a city bus cruised by to splash him from head to toe.

He tried wiping the muddy residue away, not happy

when he saw her expression. If she were a nice person, she wouldn't be laughing at him. She would be grateful. *Deeply grateful.*

"Is there a problem?" he asked, polite, thoughtful, trying to set an example. Although on the plus side, the situation did keep him from staring at her nipples.

"Nope. No problem," she answered, stifling another laugh. Then, of course, she had to cross her arms over her chest. The nipples were back.

"Good," Tyler agreed. However, he had a painful problem in his pants, and he wondered if this two-month interventional cardiology fellowship in New York was really a great idea. Of course it was a great idea. Working with Dr. Abe Keating, competing for the ACT/Keating Endowment Award. The cardiology fellowship was a chance to showcase his talents, and most of all, give him a shot at Keating's endowment, a chance to work side by side with the surgeon for another three years, doing the research that would change the way cardio-vascular surgery was done forever.

Spurred on by the drenching rain, the occasional honking car and his barely restrained sexual frustration, Tyler changed the tire in record time. He twisted hard on the wrench, tightening the nuts on the doughnut, feeling his nuts tighten with each miserable twist.

Just as he was putting the flat in the trunk, a cop car slid to a halt beside them. The officer rolled down the window.

"Need any help?" asked the officer, his eyes straying to Edie's chest.

"All done, Officer," Edie replied agreeably, possibly with a newfound respect for the law. Probably because she was driving without a proper taxi license.

"You need any help, miss?" the cop asked the criminal

cabbie, because apparently the dripping, greasy-handed cardiothoracic surgeon now looked the part of the perp.

Tyler scowled and then stepped in front of her chest. "She doesn't need anything," he told the officer, because the last thing he needed was for her to get thrown in jail. If that happened, then he'd never get to the hotel. He'd never get sex.… *Sleep*. Sleep was what he desperately needed.

The cop, sensing there was no criminal activity afoot, drove away, and Tyler and Edie climbed back in the cab. This time when she drove, Edie took the corners as slow as a grandmother, humming happily.

Tyler examined his ruined shirt, pulling it free from his pants, ready to burn the filthy thing. He looked up into the rearview mirror and met her eyes. "Why are you smiling?"

"You look good in dirt," she told him, and he noticed the dimple on the right cheek, which was completely free of both dirt and guilt.

"You're not helping."

"I'm trying to cheer you up." She sounded sincere and completely comfortable. Not painfully aroused. Not wondering what he would be like naked.

"Get me to my hotel," he growled, too tired to use his clinical voice. "That'll cheer me up."

"Why don't you like me?"

"Because you feed on people's pain."

"I do not," she insisted.

"Then why are you so intrigued by the fact that I got dumped?" It stung. Yes. Stung. Tyler wasn't used to pain. He cured pain. He prescribed meds for pain. He analyzed pain, and monitored pain, but damn it, he did not feel it. It wasn't even Cynthia so much as the idea that he wasn't good enough. It was a pain he'd stopped feeling a long time ago. Or so he thought.

"Aha, I knew I was right," Edie chirped, rubbing salt

into the wound. "Not that I'm happy you got dumped. Satisfied, yes? I mean, I do like to be right, especially about reading people. Don't you like adventures?"

Adventures were the nation's number one cause of death.

He blamed Cynthia for his foul mood. She had forced him into this embarrassing juvenile behavior. Edie had merely pummeled him until he had no choice but to regress even further.

"Sorry," he apologized politely.

"Why don't you let me buy you a drink?" she asked, apparently not sensing his still painful sexual arousal.

"Why?" he asked, stalling for time, because the first answer that leaped to mind was *yes*.

"I owe you. You're doing a nice thing, and you didn't say a word when I tooled all over the five boroughs. Tonight you've changed a flat and your girlfriend of some indeterminate amount of time dumped you, all of which happened when you should be getting well laid at the hotel. If there's anybody in the world that needs a drink, it's you. Maybe a shot of tequila, or ouzo. I know this Greek bar...."

"I don't want to go to a Greek bar," he told her, shifting uncomfortably, finding an exposed spring in the seat, feeling it cut into his thigh. Probably severing the femoral artery, thereby letting him bleed out a quick and painless death. In which case, Cynthia would have to feel bad since she had dumped him in a text message.

"How about an American bar?" Edie suggested, as if all his immediate pains could be solved with alcohol.

A bar was a recipe for disaster, but since Tyler had apparently not severed his femoral artery and was going to live, alcohol now seemed like a good idea.

"If I let you buy me a drink, one drink—will you drive me directly to the hotel?" There was a roughness in his voice that worried him. This wasn't about a drink. He should've been fantasizing about a shower, a bed. No, there were darker forces at work. Darker forces that were visualizing her. Naked in his shower. In his bed. Even naked proudly offering him one drink.

"I'll drive you straight back to the hotel. I swear," she promised, but Tyler knew when disaster lurked around the corner. He didn't like to think it was a premonition because that implied his subconscious was guiding his decision—or worse, his penis.

Tonight Cynthia had dumped him. Texas's number-four-ranked cardiothoracic surgeon with a net worth of over four million, who had saved her father's life, not once, but three times, not that anyone was counting. If there was a woman in the world who owed him the simple courtesy of a proper goodbye, it was Cynthia.

So what if he wanted to be a jackass? If he wanted to have a drink or wild sex with a woman who felt some deep-seated desire to make him feel better, then by God, he should. If he wanted to do something spontaneous and hair-raising, then he had a premeditated right to go for it.

It was because of such elaborate rationalizations that his father called him Shit-For-Brains Sophocles, but Tyler always shrugged it off. Although now he did wonder if Sophocles ever created meaningless justifications in pursuit of wild sex. Probably not. Probably Sophocles never had shit for brains. Only Tyler.

"One drink. An American bar," he agreed, resigned to his decision.

"A friend of mine works in a strip club."

He smiled at her, mud-splattered and grimy with an agenda that was just as black.

THE CLUB WAS LIKE AN underground cavern with rotating lights, an abundance of surgically enhanced body parts and a low heavy rhythm that could have aroused a dead eunuch. Identifying all the cheap marketing tactics designed to titillate him did not erase the fact that the place was getting to him.

Or maybe it was her.

Edie Higgins.

A woman with a four-hour repertoire of dirty jokes, and a body that had never been under a scalpel. The body in question had sultry curves and a rosebud tattoo that rode high on her left breast—regrettably a little too high. Yes, he was feeling shallow and a bit debauched, but in his own defense, he also acknowledged her curiously appealing joie de vivre.

The club's whiskey was overpriced and probably watered down, but it didn't matter. He hadn't touched his glass, and already he could feel himself loosening up. Her smile was infectious—in the manner of avian flu or staphylococcus, he added as an afterthought. Dr. Tyler Hart was ready to take this woman every way, any way, she'd let him.

Edie slipped an orange slice into her mouth, the juice dribbling down one side of her lip. She had luscious lips. Not collagen-full, not schoolmarm-thin. Juicy, he thought with a stupid grin, his mind wondering what her mouth tasted like. He was allergic to citrus, but was anaphylactic shock so bad? He hadn't been tested for allergies in years, and people outgrew them all the time, so theoretically, he had probably outgrown his. Tyler leaned closer, taking a deep whiff of orange and Edie, which promptly sent him into the first throes of sexual dysphoria.

"What was her name?" she asked, and he had to blink twice in order to focus on the words. *Words.*

Slowly his mind formed a suitable answer. "Cynthia." At the name, some of the sexual dysphoria evaporated.

"Cynthia," she repeated in a snotty voice and then giggled.

It made him want to smile, or maybe it was the way her

eyes tracked his face, as if he were the most fascinating man ever. His med school roommate, Ryan, had called him an alcoholic lightweight. Because of that, Tyler was usually careful when it came to drinking. Tyler lifted his full glass and took a hesitant sip.

"Was Cynthia blonde?"

"You're blonde," he pointed out, but then worried that he had a type. What if he was fatally attracted to toxic blondes? Quickly he slammed the last of his whiskey.

"I'm not a natural blonde."

"Neither was Cynthia," he volunteered in unchilvarious fashion.

Edie giggled again. This time, Tyler smiled back.

"I could buy you a lap dance," she offered, sounding so sympathetic it should have touched his heart.

You could give me a lap dance, he thought, and decided he wouldn't drink anymore. Someone needed to stay in charge. God forbid that it was her.

"Do you know why she dumped you?"

"She didn't dump me," he protested, although why he was lying he didn't know. Cynthia had dumped him. Rejected him. Humiliated him. And if he were smarter, he'd be milking this for all the sympathy points that he could get. As a specialist in coronary bypass, Tyler understood how easily the heart could be manipulated.

He lowered his head, the very picture of dejection. "You're right."

At his words, Edie put a comforting arm around his shoulders, and Tyler shamelessly moved in closer, drawn to her warmth, her generous nature, the feel of her warm and generous breasts brushing against him. Unsurprisingly, some of the sting of rejection disappeared.

"I'm sorry," she said, and once again he heard the tenderness in her voice. He was a virtual stranger, and an unchilvarous stranger at that. Before meeting Edie, he had thought that New Yorkers were hard-hearted and cynical, unmoved by the pathos of human suffering…

Except for this one.

He met her eyes. "Thank you," he told her, feeling sincere, grateful and yes, still painfully aroused.

"Do you want to meet paradise?"

"I'd love to," he agreed, his mind already transported to a lurid paradise where there was no dirt, no naked gyrating dancers…unless it was Edie. He'd let her dance. As long as she was naked. Paradise sounded perfect.

However, instead of taking his hand and leading him away from this chaos, she stood and waved her hand, gesturing wildly to one of the dancers.

Enlightenment shouldn't hurt so much.

"Is that paradise?" he guessed, as the buxom redhead bounced and buoyed her way toward him. Painful enlightenment rolled in his gut.

"What do you think?" asked Edie, looking extraordinarily pleased with herself as she started on the introductions.

"Tyler, meet Paradise, aka Anita."

Anita held out her hand, and politely Tyler shook it, not wanting to stare at what had to be 42 Double D, but somehow he knew that laws of nature and gravity had both been violated in the altering of her breasts.

"You have to be nice to Ty. I put him through crap tonight. Girlfriend dumped him, then I had a flat, which he changed in the rain by the way, and didn't even complain. Not once. He let me drive into Brooklyn, and didn't bitch about it, even though I knew he knew we weren't in Manhattan. And he's a visiting Gemini from Houston."

Her words were tribute to a man who was swimming upstream in a tide of lascivious spawn, and whose very life now depended on getting Edie Higgins out of her clothes.

Not wanting to disappoint her, Tyler adopted the humble aspect of a man who could do no wrong.

"You poor man," Anita cooed, as Edie wandered over to the bar.

The dancer moved in closer, eyelashes aflutter, and began stroking his arm.

Tyler tried to focus on her face, rather than her bare breasts, and happily noted the absence of forehead wrinkles that indicated either skin injections or a curious lack of stress in her life. He scanned the room, noted the glistening skin, the sultry dips and shakes, and knew it had to be BOTOX. If he spent every night in this place, he'd be ready for BOTOX, too.

"How do you know Edie?" he asked, finding a square of ceiling tile to concentrate on.

"We met at NYU."

"You're a student?" he asked, proudly not jumping when a dancer gyrated dangerously close to him.

"Economics."

"Of course," he answered absently, searching out Edie at the bar.

"She's a peach."

"I noticed."

"You like her?" she asked, looking at him with naked curiosity.

Tyler protested quickly. Apparently too quickly because Anita smiled with blatant sympathy. "It's okay. You don't have to feel bad. All the guys love Edie."

"Really?" he asked, noting where Edie was, leaning against the long, silver bar.

Loving Edie was bad. She was too chipper, too needy, had a well-shaped nose for trouble…*and a great ass,* he thought, leering at her skin-tight jeans.

Hastily he swallowed air.

"See the bartender?" Anita pointed toward the hulking

creature with a chain tattooed around his neck, and Tyler dragged his bleary eyes away from Edie.

"I see him."

"They had a thing a few years ago, but she dumped him."

"Who'd she fix him up with?"

Anita laughed, chucking him on the arm. "You're brighter than most."

"Thanks. So, who was the next victim?" he asked, even though he already knew. Anita was watching the chain-painted bruiser with sappy eyes. After only a few hours in the city, Tyler was now convinced that the stereotype of the hardened New York heart was flat-out wrong.

"The next victim was me." She sighed, confirming his hypothesis.

Saps. All of them.

A happy patron walked past and curved a hand over Anita's naked thigh, and she only smiled. The bartender didn't blink.

Tyler shook his head, surprised. "That's very uh, open of both of you that he doesn't get jealous."

"I'm putting him through acting school. It eases the pain."

"Yes, I get that." His eyes again found the bar, drawn to Edie immediately. In a naked sea of female perfection, the bartender was ogling the one female who was completely clothed. And Dr. Tyler Hart completely understood.

As if she sensed his weakness, Edie turned, met his eyes and smiled from across the room.

"She's not into relationships," warned Anita.

"Me, neither." Tyler watched as Edie came toward him, carrying four shot glasses. Just then the music volume increased, and a gravel-throated singer moaned about the Highway to Hell.

And tonight Dr. Tyler Hart was riding her for all he was worth.

3

EDIE WASN'T SURE WHY she'd brought him to the diner. She didn't usually reveal this part of her life to anyone. Maybe it was the Edie-induced grease stains on his hands, maybe it was the Edie-induced mud stains that had permanently ruined his pristine white shirt. Maybe, possibly, it was the arrogance in his melancholy eyes. She knew that kind of arrogance. She had lived her entire life with it, but her father had never looked that lonely. Not once.

It was after three in the morning, the darkest part of the night. Except in Manhattan, and especially at her diner. Here it was never dark, never night. Ira's had bright yellow walls, four-hundred-watt fluorescent lights and a waitstaff with dreams that didn't involve the food service industry.

After Edie ordered for them, she continued on her current mission. Trying to take the loneliness out of his eyes.

"You know, there's nothing wrong with reaching out to someone, forming a connection, even if it's temporary," she told him. Tonight she'd introduced him to Paradise, Passion, Lulu and Honey and it disappointed her that he'd turned them all down.

"I didn't say there was anything wrong with it," he insisted.

"Well, you didn't find anybody at the club," she argued, pointing out the obvious discrepancy between what he said, and what he didn't do.

"Do I look like the stripper type?" he protested, and she rolled her eyes, surprised at his cluelessness.

"Every man is the stripper type. You've just got it buried deeper than most. All that emotional repression takes time to undo."

His brows drew together. "I'm not repressed."

"You're an emotional brick, but don't feel bad. It comes from being loved by a woman named Cynthia. What did you love about her?" she asked, curious about what would attract him, since it wasn't the allure of topless females.

Carefully he arranged his silverware, silently laying out the utensils until he lifted his head and gave her a curious look. "Why do you think I loved her?"

His answer was a total dodge. She knew it. "Why were you with her, if you didn't love her?"

"Cynthia is beautiful, good company, intelligent and very fond of literature."

Oh, yawn, Edie thought to herself, so what was the source of attraction? Ha. There could be only one.

"A wildcat between the sheets," she surmised. She'd seen it before. Her old roommate, Scott had been dumped fourteen times by his girlfriend, but kept crawling back because she blew his mind—in the allegorical sense. Edie looked at Tyler sympathetically, genuinely sad that he was caught in such a web of sexual slavery. Men could be such dogs.

"I'd prefer not to discuss my sex life," he insisted, a flush rising on his cheeks.

"Sorry," she apologized. He was a cute blusher. All buttoned up and trying so very hard to be polite. Having

known her share of uncouth males, the old-fashioned gal-
lantry was new, fun...*sexy.* "Okay, we won't dwell on the
painful past of your sex life. Instead, let's concentrate on
the new and exciting future. There's a lot of women out
there. Like that one, for instance."

The waitress Edie pointed to was nearly thirty, heir to
the Petrovich fortune, and always enjoyed meeting new fab
people. "That's Olga," Edie explained, and started to wave
her over, but Tyler grabbed her hand, holding it painfully
tight.

"It's okay," he said, still holding her hand, but the tension
there became something new, nice...*warm.*

Not liking this friendlier line of thinking, Edie started
on her selling job. "Olga's great. She's so easy to talk to,
and she has this great sense of humor. Ask her to do her
Joan Rivers impression. She'll have you rolling."

"I'm sure she would, but I don't need you to take care of
me." He looked down at their entwined fingers, smiled, and
then let her hand go. And no, she didn't miss the contact.
Not at all.

"Don't take it personally," said Edie, laughing it off. "I
like taking care of people. And you're new to the city, and
you've had this miserable night, and it's completely my
fault. I'd feel ten times better if you let me do something
else for you."

"I don't want you to owe me," he insisted.

"But I do," she insisted, too.

"No, you don't. Couldn't we be...friends, just because
we actually get along?"

Get along? Trench coats and tattoos? Ties and toe-socks?
It sounded...*impossible.*

Or not?

"Maybe," she answered, then shifted uncomfortably in
the vinyl booth. "But I still feel responsible."

"You can buy breakfast. We'll call it even. Unless you can't afford it."

Edie grinned, grateful for her own financially viable position, none of which was her own doing. Dad called her a shameless loafer. Mom called it ADD. Edie merely considered herself smart. "Dad's a doc. Money is not a problem."

"What sort of doc?"

"The 'I'm bigger than God' sort of doc."

"That's no answer. They're all like that," he said seriously, and she laughed, because he seemed to understand.

"People don't understand why I don't think he's the best father ever. He's charming and funny, and his patients adore him. There are four buildings named after him because apparently three wasn't enough and—"

"Why don't you like him?"

Even though her mother understood Edie's jealousy about the time and attention he gave his patients, she never complained about his long absences from their lives. No, Clarice Higgins was a saint. Unlike Edie, who believed that saints got what they deserved. Usually an early death.

She dismissed her jealous feelings, easy squeezy. "Men don't get it. It shouldn't be so hard to do the little things. The human things. The fatherly things that fathers are supposed to do."

"But what about the good that he does? Doesn't that make up for it?"

Yes, the eternal justification for endless work hours, skipping out on birthdays, anniversaries, spoken like someone who didn't have a doc in the family. "Very few people are going to understand because they aren't the ones shut out. I don't like being shut out." She balanced her chin on her palm, needing to change the subject. "What do you do?"

"I'm taking a class."

"Where?"

"At Columbia."

She nodded. She could definitely see that, the square-jawed face with the scholarly vibe. "I love to learn. What sort of class?"

"Roman artifacts."

"Oh, that sounds so cool! Who's teaching it?"

He frowned, as if trying to pull the name out of his head. Eventually he blurted out, "Dr. Lowenbrow," looking proud of himself for remembering.

Lowenbrow? Edie checked her encyclopedic memory banks. "I don't think I know him."

"It's a big school."

"But I've taken a lot of classes," she told him, not wanting to say exactly how many.

"Haven't found one subject that sticks with you?" he asked, as if she couldn't be the egghead-student type, which was probably true.

Edie paused, not sure how much she wanted to say. She glanced at his hands, newly washed, almost back to pre-Edie status, and decided that, while she could fool him with her pseudo-intelligentsia facade, it was too early in the morning, and she'd pushed him enough. The truth seemed more appropriate. "I get bored easily."

"You just haven't found your passion yet," he said, nicely defending her as if his current opinion of her wasn't so awful. She frowned, bothered by the idea that his opinion of her might be awful, and then bothered because she was bothered.

"Life is my passion. If more people cared about people, the world wouldn't suck quite so much."

"It takes more than passion to fix things."

"It helps."

They talked over breakfast and then she ordered him a strawberry smoothie because Ira, the diner's cook, made

the best smoothies in the world. And no, strawberries
wouldn't make up for what she'd put him through tonight,
but he did seem to like the drink.

She noticed as they talked that he was cagey, not prone
to personal disclosures unless she specifically asked—
which, of course, she did. Tyler Hart was a museum curator,
specializing in antiquities. He had one younger brother,
Austen, who he wasn't sure he knew as well as he should.
Their mother was technically "missing," but Tyler assumed
that she was dead, but he didn't know for sure, and he
pretended he didn't care. In her absence, the two boys had
been raised in West Texas by their father, who was a mean
son of a bitch, and Tyler had been on only two continents,
North America and Europe, although he wanted to go to
Africa someday.

Edie explained the ins and outs of African safaris,
making him chuckle. She watched his eyes crinkle at the
corners, noticing the hypnotic swirls of brown and gold,
and was that a hint of green? Yes, she thought so. A less
self-focused individual would feel guilty about the shadows
under said sepia eyes. Or beaten themselves up because
there was a slight bloodshot tinge to them. After all, Edie
was responsible for the lot, but then he smiled at her, a
quick twitch of his mouth, and the last qualms disappeared.
Tyler Hart was different from the norm. He was too honorable. He didn't want to talk about me, me, me. And best of
all, he made her feel...well, not quite so much alone. As it
was four in the morning that was something of a miracle
for Edie.

After Olga had cleared the plates and Edie had signed
for the tab, she knew she had to drive him to the Belvedere,
and that was when the doldrums descended.

Edie navigated the streets carefully, since he'd already
had the full New York Cab Ride From Hell. After she
double-parked the cab in front of the hotel, she popped the

trunk. At first Edie tried to yank out his suitcase, but the rat wouldn't let her, and Edie, being somewhat of a closet diva, stood back and allowed him to assert his manliness.

Without thinking, she followed him a couple of steps, watching the easy confidence of his walk. Not tired, she noted, still cruising on cylinders that Edie had long burned out. Yes, he'd had eggs and she'd had pancakes, which only partially explained why a museum curator should be fully functioning after thirty-six hours of no sleep. Frankly it boggled her already-boggled mind, but then he stopped in his tracks. He wanted to pay for the cab ride from hell, which Edie politely declined. Even for Edie, taking a fare for that ride would have been way out of line.

The front of the hotel featured ornately carved gothic wood doors. If you looked closely, you would notice the various mythological creatures in *Kama Sutra* positions. Tyler seemed to be looking closely, but he didn't look quite as afraid as she would have expected. Although his museum probably had tons of porn. Those Renaissance types liked their women running naked and free—much like modern man.

She struggled to align museum curator, who saw nudity on a daily professional basis, with the buttoned-up stripper-rejecter that she had dragged around all night. Not that she needed to worry about it much. She wouldn't see him again because…

Because, she told herself firmly, and then left it at that.

His Windsor knot was now completely loose and he didn't look nearly so arrogant, nor so lonely, either, she thought, mentally patting herself on the back. Yes, there were grease stains on his shirt, but shirts could be replaced. In fact she'd buy him a new shirt and have it delivered. Something in white. "You'll be okay?"

"I'll be okay," he assured her, pulling his gaze from the door, his trench coat hanging competently over his arm.

Dawn was close, but not close enough. The night was still clinging, and Edie was hesitant to leave. "If you need anything, you can call. If you want to know the best place to get a slice, or which clubs are overpriced, or a quiet place to study."

His smile was tired, but sincere. "Tell Barnaby thanks. He needs to buy a flashlight, and there's a hole in the backseat that should be fixed."

They were goodbye words. Two strangers who would be going their own way. Being something of an expert in these words, Edie knew them when she heard them. Nervously she met his eyes, although she didn't know why she was nervous. She was never nervous, never without a smartass reply, never unable to breathe.

Tyler frowned at her, not so nervous, not so breathless, and yes, there were smartass tendencies within him as well, but they were disgustingly repressed. As such, she had no right to feel the sense of loss inside her.

"Edie?"

"Yes?"

"What are you going to do now?"

"Go back to the apartment."

He cocked his head, studying her intently. "You're not going to pick up some guy, are you?"

She couldn't help but laugh because he took everything so seriously.

"Nah. I was just kidding...." she started to explain, but her voice trailed off when she noticed the very real question in his eyes. Suddenly she wasn't feeling so non-serious anymore. In fact, the pitch in her stomach was downright serious.

A car drove by, honking at her poor parking job, but the sound was foggy and far away. Her whole world seemed foggy and far away because of the sudden pornification of her previously PG-rated brain. Now she only had thoughts of naked flesh and Windsor knots tied in untraditional locations.

Her nerves began to itch and heat in untraditional locations, as well.

"You'll be okay?" she repeated stupidly, needing to stick with easy words, and not the intricate visuals that were spinning in her head. Two bodies. Joined. Entwined. Not alone.

Tyler looked at her, disappointed. "You don't have to worry about me."

No, she wasn't worrying about him, she was *wondering* about him. Right now, she wondered about how his mouth would feel against hers. She wondered about the feel of his body shuddering above her, inside her. It was an intense sort of wonder, a liquid sort of wonder. Impulsively Edie pushed aside her goodbye words and found hello words instead. It was easier than she had expected.

"I'm not worried. A lot," she said with her best cheeky grin, which was usually termed irresistible by males and females and crotchety landlords. The man was going to be toast. "But you know, it's New York, and there are all sorts of people out there. Bad people. People that will take advantage of you. They'll milk the cab fares, make you change tires, kidnap you rather than let you go home. It's a rotten city."

"I thought you loved the city."

She lifted her shoulders, taking in the way his eyes rested on her chest, clearly noticing the way her nipples had perked up in response. "Well, sure, I love the city, but I'm tough. I know what's what. You're a—a city virgin."

It was awkward and stupid, and the most idiotic-sounding sexual come-on that she'd ever uttered.

"Not a city virgin anymore," he remarked, equally

awkward-sounding, but his eyes weren't awkward, or stupid. They were pulling her into dark, sexy places. Places that Windsor knots shouldn't know about.

"So, uh, what if somebody else comes along, and wants to take advantage of your generous nature and your tenderhearted Texas ways?"

His mouth curved up, not so tenderhearted. Some of the arrogance was back, but she didn't mind it. Much. "Maybe I'd let them," he told her, his voice pitching low, right along with her stomach. Again.

"See? What did I tell you? You've just proved my point here."

"What are you going to do now?" he asked again.

The first rays of dawn were reflecting off the windows, the rain made everything smell fresh and new and the city was coming alive. It was contagious, infectious, and she knew that she wasn't going home. Not yet.

"Now? I think I'm going to pick up somebody," she told him, lightheaded and giddy, pleased with the dawning life in his eyes, not so lonely anymore.

Tyler's suitcase landed on the sidewalk with a loud thud. "What if he's a criminal?"

"I can read his eyes," Edie answered, sure and certain. She still didn't believe in one-night stands, but if she worked very hard, she could convince herself that staying with him, laying with him, making love with him was in his best interest. The ultimate pick-me-up, in a literal sense.

"What about his eyes?"

Edie glanced over at the X-rated doors and then shook her head because there were some lies that she wouldn't perpetuate. This was one. "He belongs in the Hilton, not the Belvedere."

Undeterred, Mr. Hilton touched a finger to her mouth, sending the touch of a thousand silk feathers trickling down her spine. For the first time, Edie considered the idea that she might have misjudged him.

Nah.

Before her world completely tilted out of control, Edie picked up his suitcase and they fought over it all the way inside.

4

THEY HAD GIVEN HIS ROOM away and the next one wouldn't be ready for another three hours.

For Dr. Tyler Hart, it was the clot that burst his brain. All night, he had been so well-behaved, so thoughtful, so deserving of a single shining moment in time where the world recognized that he was not some bit of garbage that was stuck on someone's shoe.

But did the Belvedere Hotel give one good goddamn about Dr. Tyler Hart?

No. To the stuck-up clerk at the front desk, he was just another pervert needing to get his rocks off, and yes, that was true, but there were many other phrases that could have been used. Better phrases. Less demeaning phrases.

In the end, Edie grabbed his bag, grabbed his hand and they were directed to the empty bar, which didn't serve alcohol until noon because of some antiquated liquor laws. *In New York.*

"I'm sorry," she told him, apologizing for the eightieth time. "I'd offer my place, but the exterminator is scheduled today."

"It's probably for the best," he assured her, trying to make her feel better, trying to make him seem not so much the world's biggest rebounding cad, which unfortunately, wasn't a far cry from the truth.

"Probably," she agreed, which immediately ticked him off because goddamn it, he was a prize. He was a sexual stud. And perhaps, *perhaps,* he might be deficient in the romance quotient, but didn't saving lives on a thrice-weekly schedule count for something?

Oh, yeah. Not to her.

She must have noticed the frustration in his eyes, which wasn't his intent by the way, because she took his hand and rubbed her thumb along his palm. "I would have loved to have had sex with you."

She used the past tense. "Thank you," he answered politely, fighting the urge to drop down on his knees and beg. God, he needed sleep. No, he needed sex.

"I could wait around until the room is ready...."

"No—" He thrust his hands through his hair, and clunked his head down on the table, hoping he hadn't just concussed himself.

"We could find another hotel," she offered.

"No. There comes a time when you have to throw in the towel," he said, feeling the cold wood against his cheek. Then, Dr. Tyler Hart, the man who never gave up, fell into a much-needed, dreamless, sexless sleep.

WITH TYLER CONKED OUT, Edie parked the cab properly, bought a cup of coffee and then returned to the bar to watch him sleep. Gently, her fingers stroked his hair—only once—and she was pleased to see how soft it was, how the strands didn't conform to one direction or another. Of course, she could have told her the truth and offered her apartment, but Edie had rules. She didn't like to bring males home because it implied things she didn't want to imply. Not even to good, honorable men like Tyler.

She wanted to have sex with him, she wanted to watch

him without the coat, without the tie, without the grease-
stained white shirt—which she wasn't going to feel guilty
about because she would replace it. So there would be no
guilt. None at all.

Feeling guilty, Edie went to the clerk at the front desk
and used her best Manhattan sophisticate smolder. "I know
you don't have a room, but my lover is exhausted and I was
hoping we could find some place where he could sleep. He
just flew in."

"You're with Dr. Hart?"

Doctor? A Ph.D.? Really. Suddenly, she perked up. He
was like her. A student of higher learning. She should have
seen it early. He, so unassuming and humble. Not caring
about credentials or building dedications.

Now she definitely had to have him.

Driven by new inspiration and renewed lust, Edie
counted out one-two-three-four Ben Franklins under the
clerk's greedy eyes. The bills were crisp, directly from
the bank next door that she hit a few minutes ago because
cash always solved a myriad of problems. Another lesson learned from Dr. Jordan Higgins, who regularly gave
her cash in lieu of family dinners or atta-girl pats on the
back.

Edie leaned on the mahogany counter, batting her eyelashes shamelessly. "Can you do something? Please?"

The man looked left, then right, before nodding once
and sliding the bills into his pocket. "The theater is empty.
There's a bed in there."

"Theater?" Perhaps some of the shock came through in
her voice.

The clerk's look all but shouted, "amateur," and Edie
shook off her nerves. She was Edie Never-Say-Die Higgins, who was unafraid of nothing, who walked away from
nothing, who currently had a half-dead Ph.D. that needed
some Edie-love.

Amateur, my ass.

"Won't the voyeurs be disappointed in mere sleeping? Although later, perhaps..." she trailed off, brushing her knuckles on her shirt.

The clerk merely yawned. "No one is watching. The theater viewing rooms aren't open until eleven a.m. The city has ordinances."

"A pity." Edie sighed, feigning disappointment, idly glancing into the candy bowl. "I was looking forward to the experience—the freedom of giving myself over to the rites of passion in front of strangers. Oh, well. I suppose this will have to do."

She took another look into the bowl. That wasn't candy. It was condoms.

Condoms.

She picked up one, noticed the man's raised eyebrows, and then went back for seconds and thirds, stuffing them into her pocket.

The clerk penned some numbers on a slip of paper and slid it across the desk. "Here's the keycode. Through the double-doors, past the Medici hallway."

Medici hallway? Edie nodded, then pressed her fingers to her lips and kissed them, Medici style.

SOMEONE WAS KISSING his neck, and it wasn't Cynthia. Cynthia didn't believe in neck-kissing. Tyler considered opening his eyes, but he had decided he was dreaming, and he didn't want to quit the dream. Not yet.

"Tyler," whispered the dream. The dream had a low, sexy voice that tickled his ear, his neck. His cock surged, wanting its own piece of the action, but Tyler stayed still, his eyes firmly closed.

"We have a room, love. A very quiet room. So much more comfortable than this table. So much more private than this table. Wouldn't you like that? I would like that, Tyler. I want to see you, I want to feel you. I want to taste you."

One eye opened because when tasting was involved, reality was always better than a dream.

Edie.

And at that moment, he knew, deep in his cerebral cortex, that his dreams had never been this stunning.

Wanting to taste her, needing to taste her, he took her mouth and kissed her, energy flowing through him, his body firing awake in an instant. Oh, yes. This was so not Cynthia.

Edie.

She kissed him, her tongue pushing inside his mouth. Not shy. Not genteel. Never again would he hate New York.

Tyler locked his arms around her, pushing her shirt up, wanting to do more, but she laughed, put a hand to his chest.

"Follow me…" she trilled, but Tyler wasn't sure why he needed to. They had space here. They had privacy here. What more was required?

"But…" he protested, stumbling on his words, afraid that some new disaster lurked around the corner only waiting to knock him down again.

"Tyler," she said, and then he watched as she unzipped her fly, and placed his hand there.

Tyler followed.

EDIE PUNCHED IN THE KEYCODE, opened the door and dashed toward the bed. Tyler fell on top of her, a master of sexual efficiency. He kissed her mouth, her neck, one hand was pushing at her jeans, the other was groping inside her shirt, finding her breasts, and her body shook with the pleasure.

She could feel him against her. His sex was heavy, full…

and waiting. Her breath caught as that fullness ground between her thighs. There were too many layers. Too many clothes between them.

"Pants," he muttered, and voilà, her jeans were gone. She fumbled at the perfectly tailored wool slacks and marveled at how soon they disappeared. He pulled her shirt over her head, and pushed her back into the pillows, his mouth feeding on one breast, pulling, sucking, and she pressed her hips against his, because...of this.

This.

His questing fingers delved low in her panties, finding her, pushing into her, matching the persistent pressure of his dazzling mouth. Her hips followed rolling up toward his exquisite fingers, riding the strokes, because he knew exactly where to touch her. Exactly how to please her.

Tyler buried his face against her neck and sighed happily and Edie memorized that tiny sound because she knew in her heart that Tyler did not sigh happily. She'd done that for him, and she was going to make him gasp, make him come.

The first whisper of the dawn was new and full of possibilities and her hand searched the covers, finding the condoms, grasping one, and trying to rip it open. Sensing her frustration, possibly due to her colorful vocabulary, he took it from her, and she could feel him moving, adjusting and then...

Yes.

The aching in her stilled when he filled her, so thick, so hard, so good.

So perfect.

The air burned, her whole body flush with the heat, until he rose above her, putting a long distance between them. Those steady eyes settled on her face, studying her before he sighed again. Not so happily this time.

"Why are you here?"

Edie froze at his responsible tone, wondering if this was a trick question, hoping it wasn't because he felt so good, so right. But, alas, all that goodness slid out of her. Alone again.

Foolishly, she pushed at his hair even though it was too short to be in his eyes. She wanted to touch the dark strands that hung low on his face. Wisely she knew that this wasn't the time.

Dammit.

Edie sighed, not so happily, either. Although she couldn't blame him. In fact, she should have expected it. In fact, before he had made her forget that she expected it, she had expected it. And prepared for it, as well.

Not so prepared now, are we?

She smiled her fly-by-night smile that said no big deal, and pulled out the standard Edie Higgins script. "We're having a connection, a momentary joining of two bodies who have stumbled across each other, groping in the darkest of nights, moving toward some feeling of soulful humanity."

"Fuck," he muttered, rolling off her and her soulful humanity.

"Well, that is one way of stating it. Two animals copulating in a primitive ritual of procreation and species sustainability. Although the condom takes care of most of that."

He turned his head, and met her eyes, and she hated the maturity there, the practical wisdom that saw past her words.

"Why are you here?"

Edie rolled to her side of the bed, her hands knotted in the ruby spread. "I wanted to feel better. That's all. Sue me."

The room was so quiet that she could hear the exhale of his lungs, the shifting against the covers, away from her. Rejecting her.

Slowly she opened her eyes, watching them in the mirrored ceiling above the bed, her eyes a little too bright, her smile a little too flip and her hair a little too casually messed. There were so many differences between them, so why did it hurt? Consistency wasn't a fixture in Edie's life—unless someone needed her for something. Everything in her life was part of the universal economy of bartering. Something given, something taken in return. Now Tyler wanted to disrupt her system. Tyler, the scrupulous keeper of scruples. Even without the trench coat and tie, he was who he was. Not the sort who traded favors easily. His chest was broad, strong. His legs reliable, the kind that changed tires in the rain. Legs that didn't collapse no matter how much shit she piled upon him.

"I don't want you to owe me." His words were spoken quietly, but they were a lot better than what she had imagined. Edie rolled a few inches closer.

"Why are *you* here?" she asked, curious what had finally broken him down. Wounded pride? Exhaustion?

Or Edie?

"It's my room," he answered, which was no answer at all. Gingerly he lifted himself on his elbows, scanned the velvety bordello furnishings and then collapsed back into the pillows. "I'd hoped it was my room. Is this my room?"

"For now," she hedged, not wanting to say more, waiting for him to say more, which he didn't.

"Why are you here?" she asked again, needing to know. People were simple, motivated by basic pursuits. They didn't forgo pleasure easily. They didn't forgo happiness—usually. Before she laid down her cards, he was going to have to have a little more skin in the game. The important kind, not the naked kind.

Tyler moved closer and touched her, skimming one gentle finger down her arm. It was a nice touch, but a careful touch. "I want this. I want you. For most of this night, I've willingly followed you through hell, panting like a dog. I imagined you above me, below me, surrounding me. I'm pretty much at the end of my rope."

As declarations went, it was first-rate, but the truth was in the deeds. "So why did you stop?"

"Why are you here?" he countered.

It was easier to stare up at the mirrored ceiling and look into her own manic eyes than to tell him the truth. The room was full of illusions of infinite spaces, of walls that didn't exist. It didn't matter what she said. It didn't really matter why she was here, or why he was here. The fact was, they were. Two people primed for sex, sharing a stage set for sex.

So why waste it talking?

This time there were no doubts when she climbed onto the welcoming hips. Dark power pulsed through her as she pushed her fingers through his mass of dark hair, mussing it nicely. Next, she leaned low, her mouth brushing his, her breasts brushing against him, a touch that she so badly needed right now.

"For this," she whispered, skimming her tongue across the seam of his mouth, meeting his lips.

"For this," she said, cupping his large hands over her breasts, reveling in their warmth.

Then she lowered herself on top of his cock, clenching tightly, sighing deep. "For this," she purred.

Slyly she began to rock, watching his eyes—serious, steadfast—and feeling her muscles quiver with pleasure as much as exhaustion. Her smile turned wanton, the same thing that all men craved, but his gaze stayed steady. Quickly she looked away.

Edie wanted to move fast, race for the orgasm, but his hands locked around her, setting a slower pace, a seductive pace, and in spite of herself, Edie felt herself relaxing, falling into the rhythm. There was nothing but the heavy fill and release.

He was as silent as she, one hand brushing against her lips, and she took his finger in her mouth, pleased with the intense flash in his eyes, pleased with the sudden jerk of his hips.

Weakness at last.

It was in everyone, even the buttoned-up scrupulous types who didn't belong here.

Showing his true colors at last, he rolled her on her back, raising her legs, pushing deep into her. Her gaze drifted over his shoulder to the ceiling, watching them, watching him move inside her. With each thrust, she could see the sure flexing of his buttocks, the strong arch in his back and the vulnerable bend in her legs. Legs that were open and begging to be used.

She didn't have to wait long. Tyler rose up higher, moving faster, his big chest heaving, and she watched one drop of sweat slide down his torso. It was like flying, the pressure building inside her. She was so close to coming, so close to the end. All she needed was one inch higher, one minute further, but then...

Tyler slid out of her, glancing up at the ceiling, and there was a steeliness in his jaw, a rigid bend in his spine. Unbreakable. Impassable.

No.

His hands were rough as he spread her legs farther apart, not so controlled anymore. She waited, breathlessly watching as he lowered his head between her thighs. Men didn't pleasure Edie. Edie pleasured men, but not here. Not with him.

When his mouth settled on her, the room began to spin, and her fingers reached out, looking for purchase. He was all that she had. Her hands locked at the base of his neck, first pushing him away, then pulling him close, anticipating each lick.

This wasn't fair. Sex was pleasure. It was the giving and taking of parts, not identities, not hearts, not souls. It scared her that he wanted things from her. Apparently Tyler Hart was not content with parts. *Nice* men never were. It was why she usually avoided them, until tonight. Until this.

Mindlessly she rolled her head from side to side and the red covers of the bed seeped into her blood, into her mind. Her fingers clenched until she knew they would break, but his relentless assault continued, and she heard the plaintive echoes of her own gasps, her pleas, until she stopped fighting, because in the end, it was Edie who always gave way.

Her body screamed, muscles shuddering, but he wouldn't leave her alone. When the orgasm came, it broke her in two.

Tyler moved up her body, and she knew there was more, it was there in his face, the determined glint in his dark eyes, no longer scholarly or unshakable. Now he was a man with one goal. Her. Edie took a sharp breath, her blood starting to rise, and instinctively her body arched toward him, surrendering to the call. He took her, no longer cool, no longer controlled, and she smiled up at him, urging him to take his pleasure.

Of course he did, and Edie welcomed the dark pain, the sharp slap of skin and sweat. She watched the steely gaze melt under fire, just as she had hoped.

His powerful thrusts never slowed, never faltered, taking her to climax simply because he could. She stopped feeling, stopped falling, and simply let herself ride.

This was no more than pleasure, no more than parts.

Finally, when his body was slick with sweat, when the scarlet spread had darkened to a well-used red, when the musky smells of sex surrounded them, Tyler rose on his knees, muscles frozen, and it was the ultimate turn-on, the ultimate aphrodisiac.

With a sly smile, Edie watched as Dr. Tyler Hart, man of trench coats and scruples, lost them all and fell to earth.

A PHONE WAS RINGING somewhere below. Tyler opened one eye and felt a soft breast underneath his cheek. Instantly he snapped awake, ready to perform long, intricate procedures, ready to save lives, ready to confront whatever needed his attention.

No, he thought, looking around. This was his hotel.

The phone beeped again and Tyler picked it up, and pressed the button, already prepping himself for the required professional response.

"Tyler?"

A woman emerged from the covers like some pagan goddess, lean and tasty, and he remembered that taste. Warm saliva pooled in his mouth.

"Tyler?" repeated the voice on the phone and he shot out of bed, fumbling for both clothes and sanity. Finding neither.

Finally abandoning all pretense of professional response, Tyler turned off the phone and collapsed on the floor.

"Who was that?" asked the seductive voice that had haunted what he thought was a dream. That smooth voice had teased him, tormented him, slayed him.

Tyler looked up, seeing the reflection in the godforsaken mirrored ceiling, and then swallowed hard.

"Cynthia. I'm almost positive it was Cynthia."

5

"CALL HER."

The naked woman in the bed was telling him to call his girlfriend, former girlfriend, *ex-girlfriend?* What was the correct vernacular for this particular nightmare?

Normally, Tyler was not affected by nudity. He'd seen old nudity, young nudity, dead nudity and baby nudity. But this felt personal. It was his nudity. Betrayal nudity.

Yet even racked with guilt, he still managed to notice Edie's hotness. He could still remember the feel of her muscles tightening around him, her fingers digging into his back. "I'll call her later," he told the naked woman.

"Go on. I'll help you," Edie encouraged, as if completely comfortable with the situation.

Her eyes were alert and gleaming with diabolical purpose, and it finally dawned on Tyler that Edie Higgins was not as aimless as she had first appeared. Apparently, Tyler was now her purpose. First, it had meant seducing him. Now it was repairing his relations with his girlfriend, ex-girl— *Cynthia.* For a split second his mind puzzled over those two seemingly incongruous directives, but then the red velvet spread slipped a few inches lower. His bleary gaze was drawn to a long sliver of golden skin and Tyler was struck by two seemingly incongruous directives: wanting to bed Edie again, and wanting to fall back into his former peaceful life.

"I think I'm going to get dressed," he announced, hoping she'd get dressed, as well. Surprising no one, Edie chose to ignore his hint and instead watched him pull on his pants with those brown eyes. Tyler buttoned his shirt, feeling helplessly exposed, but then he noticed the knowing smile playing at the corners of her mouth, and in a moment of rebellion, he left it hanging brazenly undone. Childish? Yes.

Courageously he punched in Cynthia's number.

"Tyler?"

Tyler cleared his throat, turning away from the allure of the woman on the bed. "Yes? You called?"

"I'm sorry."

"Not a problem."

"I owe you an explanation," Cynthia said, talking as if Tyler was the victim. And actually, he reminded himself, he was the victim. He was the injured party in this whole blasted experience. Tyler straightened his shoulders and began to walk the room, listening quietly while Cynthia carried on.

"I did something terribly wrong, and you didn't deserve it, and I shouldn't have, but sometimes I want to…*feel*. I want to reach out and grab life, and…I could never do that with you. He was there, and it was stupid, and I knew it was stupid, but I did something stupid, something wild and crazy and Tyler, I realized I should have done ended things with you a long time ago."

Cynthia had cheated on him? She had hedonistic, indulgent, awesome sex with someone else? And *that's* why she had broken up with him?

"Say something," Cynthia begged. "You're mad, aren't you? You're disappointed with me."

Disappointed? Tyler considered that one, and rejected it. "I'm not disappointed with you, Cynthia," he offered, which was completely honest. *Relieved* was probably the more precise description. He felt a gentle tap on his back, and when he turned around, Edie was there, no sheet covering her, because apparently flagrante delicto was the best way to resurrect his conscience.

Tyler tried to look away from her, but ten million years of male evolution had created a male-cornea female-aureole neural pathway that would not be denied.

Stay in the moment. Wounded Animal. Victim.

Now feeling more in control, he muted the phone. "Yes?"

"What's going on? What did she do? Are you okay?" And yes, Edie seemed entranced. Not by sexual hypnosis, but human drama. His human drama.

"She didn't do anything. There's nothing going on."

Edie didn't believe him for a second. "Oh, come on. You can tell me. Let me help."

"She made a mistake," he admitted, caving to the lure of her sparkling eyes and rose-tatted breast. Actually, the tattoo was fairly good work, small, with elaborate details, tiny thorns, and a deep pink that matched the pink of her...

"Oh," Edie began and then her eyes grew large. "*Really?* She cheated? That's so cool." Noting the dark look on his face, she quickly rephrased. "Well, not cool, but it speaks a lot to her humanity, and her insecurities."

Only Edie would see a mistake as a badge of honor. "Personally I think her humanity stinks."

"Yeah, sure..." Her outstretched hand encompassed the bordello bed, the massacred sheets and, most painful of all, Tyler's Moral High Ground... "But in light of everything, this way you get a free ride. Pardon the pun. Have you thought about what to say?"

"I have nothing else to say to her. It's done." There was

no pain, no hurt, just a numbing sense of it being over. He glanced at Edie's not so numbing body. And there was lust. Don't forget the lust.

Edie met his eyes and he could imagine the wheels turning. "Does she want to get back with you?" Then she whacked herself on the forehead. "What the heck? Of course she wants to get back with you. She wants to start anew, rebuilding your trust, using this as a chance to add new support to a previously faltering relationship."

It was fascinating to watch her analytical skills at work. All of Edie Higgins's attention was laser-focused on understanding Cynthia. And why? What possible purpose did she have for that? Unless she was truly invested in healing Cynthia's pain? Seriously?

Seriously?

Tyler dismissed the thought. And once again, Edie had sucked him into her universe. Lack of sleep. It was the only explanation, and Tyler quickly reined in his wandering focus.

Tyler unmuted the phone. "Cynthia? Sorry."

"It's all right. I know you're busy. I should have waited until you got back."

"I'm glad you didn't," he told her sincerely.

"Do you mean that?"

"I do."

"Tyler, what do we do? I don't think we can go back to where we were."

"No," he told her flatly.

"You don't want to go forward?"

"You sent me the text message," he pointed out.

"I know, but…no, you're right. I love you, Tyler."

Tyler found a nearby wall to support himself. A wall that was trimmed with cavorting nymphs and promiscuous pagan creatures, none of whom cared about moral high ground, or upstanding models of behavior. And each of those devious little creatures was currently watching him, saying, "Hallelujah."

"I need to go."

"Yes. I'm sorry, Tyler."

"Goodbye," he told her and ended the call. That was that.

TYLER HART WAS NO LONGER buttoned-up. Edie had accidentally-on-purpose contributed to that. And now there was a sadness in his eyes that he didn't deserve. She reached out, wanting to touch him, wanting to tell him she'd screwed this one up. However, Edie knew there'd been enough Tyler-touching to last a lifetime. It wasn't the time to add to her mistakes.

Normally, Edie's machinations served the common good, but sometimes—this time—she'd been too caught up in her own issues. She had finally been with someone who didn't need to use her, and it had confused her, made her miss important things. Usually the people who she affected deserved what they got. But not Tyler.

Determined to begin anew, determined to make this one right, Edie got her clothes, dressed with lightning speed and then stood next to him in that friendly, buddy, pal sort of way. It didn't help that his cologne was not the friendly, buddy, pal sort of stuff. It was simple, clean, subtle. Everything that wasn't her.

"I'm sorry." Apologizing was easier and more heartfelt than she expected. Humility did not usually sit well with the Higgins family.

He stared at her, and she saw the surprise in his face. "You don't need to be sorry."

A lesser person would have taken that and run with it, but Edie needed to do more. She owed him more. "I do. You wouldn't be here if not for me. You're not that guy. I've treated you badly. I purposefully set out to seduce you only because I didn't want to be alone, and if I hadn't done that, you'd be happily talking to your no-longer ex-girlfriend and making things right."

His smile was lopsided and so very, very tired. "She did cheat on me."

Edie scoffed because in Tyler's world mistakes were a Big Freaking Deal. In Edie's world mistakes were a part of life. But she admired his world, and she wouldn't suck him into hers. Again.

"Don't be so rough on her," Edie said gently. There was hope for these two crazy kids. All they needed was a little push in the right direction and a little Super-Glue, and everything would be okay again.

"We're done."

"I'm sorry," she apologized again, pulling his tie off the bedside lamp, straightening it, memorizing it. He took it from her, buttoned his shirt and began retying the knot, and she was glad to see a lot of the older Tyler returning.

"Do I have a room?" he asked when she handed him his boots, noticing they weren't quite as impeccable as the rest. She took the spread and worked at the leather, trying to create an impeccable shine. Better. Not great, but it'd do.

She watched as he restored his clothes and smoothed down his hair, and like magic, the steel was back in the jaw, scruples and honor were back in his eyes, exactly where they belonged. "I'm sure your room is ready. I'll hit the road and let you get your life back in order." She wanted to be perky and not so clingy, and she forced a brilliant smile to her face before picking up her bag and slinging it over her shoulder.

When she got to the door, he stopped her with a hand to the arm. "Edie. Thank you."

She glanced at his hand, feeling his touch burn through

clothing, through regrets, through all the good intentions that she wanted to keep. "Thank you? For what?"

"For last night. I hurt. It felt good. You were being nice."

It took a decent man to find something redeeming in her actions. "It was good?"

"It was good," he repeated, then noticed his hand on her arm and promptly removed it.

"Thanks."

She opened the door, confident that she was going to walk out of this room that was now swimming with lost ideals, and morning-after regrets, and flashbacks of two bodies moving together as one.

"Edie? Can I see you again?"

In his eyes, hidden among the honor and scruples was vulnerability and desire, neither of which were smart at the moment. Calmly she told herself that she wasn't going to take advantage of him. He needed to move on to his museum project and to starched blond females named Cynthia, or Buffy, or Penelope. He should be free to wear his Windsor knots without her scheming and toying and in general screwing things up for him.

"You think that's a good idea?" That was as close to No as she could get.

"I think it's one of the worst ideas I've ever had," he admitted.

"And you hate admitting that, don't you?"

He nodded. "You have no idea how humbling it is."

"I like you, Tyler Hart. You're such a big lug of ego, but you do it so much nicer than my dad."

"I'm very glad to hear that."

He just stood there, and it was the most powerful not-touching she'd ever known. Something about him pulled at her, the buzzing electron orbiting a solid nucleus, helpless to move away from that magnetic, positive charge. The laws of quantum mechanics, much like the laws for foolish people, could not be denied. But maybe she could be a little wiser.

"I can't see you again," she said, and she was very proud of herself for actually forming the words.

Not sensing her weakness, or perhaps to take advantage of it, he slowly moved toward her. There was a reckless gleam in his eyes that scared her…that aroused her.

"You're so good at saying what you don't mean." His voice was gruff, raw, probably from lack of sleep, too much emotion. All Edie's doing.

"You're not my type." She turned away from to study the walls, the bed, the marauding wood nymphs.

He came up behind her, pressing her against him and her eyes drifted closed.

"I could be your type," he whispered in that husky voice, taunting her, seducing her. Edie leaned into the strong arms, the reliable torso, the unshakable erection.

"I don't get involved," she answered in a very shakable voice.

"We could be—" his teeth nipped at her ear "—friends."

Friends. The word was so rife with potential. Her loins quivered at the thought.

"You don't understand the female mind," she protested, which wasn't a very compelling argument, but his mouth was against her neck, and his hands were wandering beneath her shirt, and frankly, it was a miracle she could think at all.

"Teach me," spoke the honorable man who was slowly bringing her over to the dark side. "Show me what you want."

Those nimble fingers moved lower, unzipping her fly, slipping beneath her panties and then slipping between her thighs. *Slipping* being the optimal word because Edie's dark side was nefariously wet, having been convinced the first time he'd laid hands on her. "It's not easy," she breathed. "It's an...*ohhhh*...intricate pro-pro-pro-cess."

"I live for intricate processes," he whispered, his persuasive mouth skimming over her neck. Meanwhile, down below, his fingers were taking their own liberties, stroking and skimming, and for one blissful moment, she reveled in the touch. Then her conscience kicked in. She needed space, distance...*a working brain,* none of which was happening until she...

Untangled him from her and put her clothes regrettably back to rights. Quickly she took a long, safe step away.

His hair was deliciously tousled, his eyes were temptingly hot, and...

Working brain. Working brain.

She stood there, drawing in deep breaths, getting the oxygen flow started once again. The door was there, so close. *Go, Edie.* But because she needed to touch him one last time, Edie tweaked his tie and laughed. "Get cleaned up, get some rest. Lessons start on Saturday."

6

TYLER WAS HAVING A DREAM. He was in surgery. Dr. West-book, the chief of cardiology was there, as well as the batty surgery nurse whose name he never remembered. Everyone was staring at Tyler because he was naked, but he didn't care, yet why didn't he care? Now Tyler was fighting to wake up because his pager was buzzing, and...

It was his phone.

"Ty? You're getting lucky? Wait. Don't tell me. If Cynthia is there, say 'I am not getting lucky.'"

It was only Austen. His brother. His pain-in-the-ass brother who rated only slightly more higher than a naked-surgery nightmare. "I'm not getting lucky," he snapped, peeking under the leopard-striped sheets, pleased to local-ize his boxers. No naked here.

Not anymore.

"Cool! And now Cynthia's looking at you all soft and sexy, but you can thank me for that later. Do you love the hotel?"

The hotel. The night. *Edie.* Memories flooded his mind, every smell, every touch, every truly awesome touch. Un-fortunately, he was now fully erect, facing substantial brain blood-loss, and had to converse with his...*brother.*

Difficult, but not impossible. Tyler lived for the impossible. "I hate the hotel."

"To that, I say—why didn't you move to the Hilton? *I know you.* Secretly, you suppress these wild impulses. But this way, you have an excuse to cut loose. Best of all, you don't have to feel guilty because it's all my fault."

So why didn't Tyler move to the Hilton? It wasn't too late. He could move to the Hilton, but then Austen would be right. Then Edie would be right. Everyone would see him as an emotional coward who chose to run when surrounded by the garish, in-your-face sexual stimuli. And they'd all be right, but if he changed hotels, then they'd know it.

Leopard sheets were preferable.

"Does this cheap chicanery work with the state senators? If so, I really need to rethink my voting choices."

"You wouldn't believe how often it works. I am simply the voice of sin and temptation."

"You are the voice of Beelzebub." True, his brother was a complete pain, but Austen was his only brother, and theirs was a brotherhood united—although it didn't mean they had to agree.

"The hotel worked for you, didn't it, Romeo? What does Cynthia think of the place? I bet she's impressed with this more spontaneous, more sexual version of yourself?"

"She didn't come," Tyler admitted, at which point Austen groaned.

"Oh, dude...what are you thinking? Only of yourself and your own satisfaction? Keep that up and she's going to be on the first flight back to Houston."

If only it were that simple.

"Cynthia's not in New York. She broke up with me." He rubbed his head. "It's a long story."

"You okay?" his brother asked, now appropriately serious.

"I'm fine."

"You sound fine. Why do you sound fine? Broke up? As in really, truly, not-gonna-call-at-two a.m. broke up?"

"Yes."

"What did you do to her?" asked his previously caring brother.

"Why does this have to be my fault?"

"Because you're cold. I hate to tell you, but you're not the world's most sensitive guy, Tyler."

"I am not cold," insisted Tyler, getting tired of people pointing out his flaws. He didn't have a lot of flaws. He worked very hard not to have flaws, and people needed to appreciate that. Especially his brother.

"You're as sensitive as a brick. You don't get women. They need...delicate handling."

Tyler was an expert at delicate handling. "I know that. This isn't my fault. She cheated."

"Because you drove her into another man's arms," responded his brother, making Tyler the responsible party.

"Go to hell."

"Listen, it's either that or your bedside manner isn't all it's cracked up to be. So which is it, bro? Unsatisfactory sex or you're a brick?"

Tyler considered his choices. "I don't think I'm that bad," he finally replied, although now he was wondering if maybe his brother was on to something. Edie had said the same thing. Cynthia had broken up with him....

Damn.

"You're emotionally stunted. It's all Frank's fault. We both are. I'm just better with the ladies."

Tyler could be better the ladies if he truly applied himself. He had heroic qualities. More heroic qualities than Austen. All he needed to do was apply himself, and maybe with some guidance... Slowly, Tyler smiled. Guidance from *Edie*. She had offered—yes, it was all garbage, and she knew he knew it was garbage, but the offer was still on the table. Guidance and sex. Edie loved to help people, loved to impart her wisdom to whomever would listen, and to be fair, she did seem to know her way around the male-female dynamic.

It was a win-win. He'd get practical relationship advice, and cock-busting sex, as well. And Edie would get the reinforcement that she needed.

"Don't kid yourself, Austen. I'm fine with the ladies."

"Good, because you're in New York City. Alone. Single. You should live it up. Be free and unattached. I know. I'll fly up."

"No."

Brotherhood only went so far. Austen loved fun. Tyler loved work. Austen loved wild, impetuous, meaningless sex, and Tyler would go to the grave before his brother discovered that Tyler had discovered that Tyler did, too. Good God, if Austen guessed, then he would want to carouse together like some low-budget buddy flick. Tyler shuddered at the thought.

"Think about it. Your birthday is in a couple of weeks. We could celebrate in the city. Two brothers, small-town cowboys making their way in the urban jungle. Lost and alone."

"We're not cowboys," Tyler corrected, knowing that correcting his brother was a mistake, however, such permanently conditioned behaviors were impossible to stop.

"But do the women of New York know we're not cowboys? I think not." Nonsensical statements such as that were the primary reason that Tyler needed to stop correcting his brother.

"Stay home," Tyler pleaded.

"Ha-ha. Don't want the competition, do you? Think that all the women will ignore you if I'm in the room sucking up all the sexual oxygen?"

"Screw you, Austen."

"Now *that's* the brother I know and love."

Tyler noticed the time and realized he'd only had two hours' sleep. He blinked rapidly a few times and decided that he'd carried family obligation far enough. "Why are you calling?"

"To annoy you."

"No. There's some other purpose because it's seven a.m. in Texas, and you're never up before nine."

"Can't I just call and shoot the shit with my big bro?"

"No, that would imply sensitivity and thoughtfulness on your part."

"That's it. Now I'm definitely flying up there, Ty."

"Why are you calling?"

"No reason."

"Seriously?"

"Seriously," Austen insisted. "There is no reason."

"Seriously?" Tyler asked, not believing it for a second.

"Seriously, seriously. No reason."

At last Tyler knew. Lack of sleep, jet lag and wild, meaningless, *really great sex* had dulled his normally razor-sharp mind. "She called?"

"She called," Austen admitted, sounding only a little deflated, and thankfully, he didn't question why Tyler hadn't figured it out earlier.

"That's why you want to fly up here," Tyler persisted, keeping on the offensive because Austen would stay silent for only so long. Brooke had called Tyler as well, but he didn't tell Austen these things because it was easier to pretend that Brooke didn't exist.

"I don't want to fly up there," Austen argued.

"You just said you did."

"I lied."

"So stay home," Tyler suggested.

"Tricky, very tricky. Trying to corner me into admitting the truth."

"You couldn't admit the truth if seventy cheerleaders attacked you in Jell-O."

"Tyler! Listen to you. Making the sex jokes as if they don't make you twitchy and uncomfortable. It's the hotel, isn't it? I should come see it. Check it out for myself."

Tyler wasn't fooled. There were very few things that Austen dodged. Truth, lasting commitment and the harsh reality of their mother. Tyler, being a rational medical professional, had long understood that their mother had a reason for walking out the door. She had a reason for abandoning them to the paternal pile of bitterness that was their father.

Only eight-year-old Tyler had been there to see her leave. Only eight-year-old Tyler had been there to cry and plead and try to change her mind.

In the end, he hadn't been persuasive enough, caring enough, or cute enough, and life went on. That was water under the bridge and their mother wasn't worth the time, thought, or pain.

"Why don't you just admit your weakness? You want to see her." Tyler said the words easily, because he didn't care about his sister. She was a stranger and wouldn't be a part of their lives because the Hart family had only two members; Tyler and Austen. "You want to see her because you want to know what she's like, or if it's all a big con."

Austen blew a raspberry into the phone. "Sure it's a con. Dad would have said if Sheila was pregnant when she left us. He would have called her a no-account whore, and then bitterly explained how if she'd been pregnant, the little brat wasn't his."

"Maybe he didn't know," Tyler suggested, as if the thought had only just occurred to him.

"Nah. Frank knew every bad thing about her. He was

very talented that way, almost eerily so. No way that he could have kept it secret. It's a con meant to separate me from my millions."

"You don't have millions," Tyler reminded him, merely to get his brother back on Planet Earth.

"I don't have millions *yet,* but my future income potential is limitless. After I convince the East Texas legislators that drilling for natural gas in somewhat porous shale is not only financially viable, but a boon to the state economy, then, as God is my witness, the red Ferrari will be mine."

Tyler leaned back against the leopard-striped pillows, making himself comfortable now that he was once again firmly in control of his life. Which was exactly where he needed to be.

"Stay home. We're not going."

"You're dying to go, aren't you?" Austen shot back, the irrepressible irreverence clear in his voice. "I think you're missing the opportunity of a lifetime here, Tyler. She's there. You're there. It'd be easy for me to hop on a plane and join you, we'll take a car to Cold Springs. It's perfect."

"No. Forget it. I need to get to the hospital," Tyler stated firmly, because there were things that were best left unknown.

Austen argued for a little bit longer, but eventually gave up, and after Tyler put down his phone, he noted the tranquility of the hotel room. The palatial bed complete with Arabian knights canopy, the glass stripper pole, the supersize hot tub, and in the midst of such blatant, cheap sexuality, he felt a sense of foreboding because Tyler was already aching to see Edie Higgins again. Feel her legs locked around him, feel her tongue in his mouth, around his cock.

Quickly, he showered and dressed in a neatly pressed suit, complete with an impeccable Windsor knot. By the time he'd left the garish hotel, Tyler was in perfect control again.

Yeah, right.

THE SIDEWALK IN FRONT OF the hospital was buzzing with picketers, nurses marching with handmade signs, chanting catchy union jingles such as "Terminal wages, terminal care," "Sucky wages, Sicky patients" and the one which Edie had proudly created herself—"A poorly paid nurse is a pain in your ass."

Although Edie believed in better wages for society's caretakers, she wasn't there because of it. Primarily, Edie believed that the health-care industry's blood lust for profit had erased the word *care* from health care, which was way too wordy to fit on a sandwich board. Or, alternatively, she could have been there because the hospital was St. Agnes', which happened to be where Dr. Jordan Higgins worked.

Across the street, Edie's mother was holding a Bloomingdale's bag. A darkening scowl creased her face. Clarice Higgins didn't support Edie's more militant leanings. Completely undeterred by such apathy, Edie waved cheerfully, which only deepened her mother's scowl. Of course, today was her parents' wedding anniversary, and if Edie were in her mother's Jimmy Choos and knew her husband wouldn't be home until the crack of dawn, then Edie would probably be scowling, too.

Not wanting to cause her mother more undue stress, Edie motioned the union rep over and planned her retreat. "Thanks for coming to us at the last minute, doll," the woman told her. "What hospital did you say you're from?"

"St. Jordan's," Edie improvised.

"Never heard of it. Want to put in a few more hours? Lacey needs a break, and the Jersey union hasn't shown. Probably still at lunch, the lazy dogs."

"Give me a sec and I'll ask," Edie said, returning her sign to the woman's well-motivated hands. "My mother is across the street. She only has one kidney and it's not good for her to be out in the heat. Malpractice, the bastards. Very sad. It's the reason I went to nursing school. To prevent these sorts of medical screwups, and to keep the focus on the sick, rather than those hotshot Hollywood docs who have egos bigger than the sun."

The woman nodded with sisterly solidarity, then bumped Edie's fist, and waved her off. "Go be with your mother. You never know how long you have. God go with you, and remember—kicking ass for the nursing class."

Now officially free, Edie jogged over to where her mother was waiting, her Jimmy Choos tapping with the amazing power of the truly upset. "I thought you were going to see your father. Did you pick this meeting spot on purpose?"

"Who? Me?" asked Edie, blinking innocently.

"I take it your father didn't see you picketing?"

"No."

Her mother shot a disgusted glance at the hospital. "Damn."

Edie smiled, pleased to see that beneath the five-thousand-dollar powder-blue suit, beneath the five-hundred-dollar protein hair treatments, beneath the 24-karat gold-plated exterior was the still beating heart of the woman who had danced naked at Woodstock.

"Mom, you little anarchist. You've been reading Karl Marx for book club again, haven't you? Should I tell Dad?"

Her mom tipped her Gucci glasses downward, shooting Edie a death-laser look. "You do, you die."

"So where are we going for lunch?"

"Someplace with fabulous desserts. Saks?"

"Sounds fab. What are you getting for your anniversary

this year?" asked Edie, spying the blue Tiffany's bag. At her mother's signal, a cab instantly appeared.

In short order, they were settled in the backseat and jetting off for 5th Avenue. Edie's mother nodded toward the bag. "Diamond bracelet and matching necklace," she whispered.

"Dad's got great taste," Edie whispered back, knowing that her mother had picked it out, and not quite understanding why her mother didn't protest more. Clarice Higgins was a great human being, as worthy as Edie's father, and yet somehow, when weighed on the scales of Jordan Higgins's priorities, her mother always ended up with the shaft.

"Don't be snide, Edie. It doesn't reflect well on my parenting skills."

"Hey, Dad married you. He's not all bad."

Her mother patted Edie's thigh. "That he did. So let's go spend his money."

"We could have champagne."

"Two glasses each," added Clarice with what could almost be termed a giggle.

The Friday afternoon traffic was stop-and-start, and Edie didn't mind, although she did give their driver instructions to the shortcut on Eleventh Avenue, which, *of course,* he ignored. While they sat in traffic, Edie studied her mother, checking for signs of worry, stress or displeasure.

She knew that a small part of her mother's not-quite-storybook life was due to her daughter's possibly not-quite-storybook behavior, but comforted herself with the knowledge that her father at least made Edie look like the World's Bestest Daughter Ever.

"Did Dad even remember?" Edie asked, just as any dutiful daughter would.

"His secretary sent me flowers and a card."

"So thoughtful of Mary Helen."

"I thought so."

There was a long awkward silence wherein Edie considered withholding any comment, but eventually her sense of emotional injustice was so overwhelmed that the words burst free.

"Why do you do it, Mom?"

Clarice Higgins, accustomed to her daughter's overwhelmed sense of emotional injustice, smiled patiently. "I love him. He's a doctor. The world demands certain sacrifices from women who marry into the military or medicine."

Edie shrugged uncomfortably because in Edie's worldview, Clarice Higgins and Edie Higgins were not meant to live in the shadow of greatness. Every human being had great potential—sometimes untapped—but that didn't make them superfluous.

"Whatever."

"How's the job at the diner?" her mother asked, neatly changing the subject.

For a long moment, Edie considered telling her mother that she'd actually purchased the diner eight months ago, and that it was turning a nice profit for the Women's Education Project and that the morning cook, Wanda, was now studying to become a teacher and that they had a break-in last week and someone had cleaned out the register. Edie thought it could have been Marjorie, her previous cook who had some personal issues, mostly due to a fondness for certain illicit pharmaceuticals, but she wasn't convinced that Marjorie had the necessary ambition for a life of crime. Her mother looked at her, expecting no miracles from her daughter because Edie had never really dazzled. When Edie did decide to divulge the details of her life to her parents, she wanted to wow them, amaze them, dazzle them with her greatness.

In the big scheme of things, owning a diner was not big news in the Higgins family. There was only room for one model of godlike deitude in the Higgins family, and Edie wasn't it.

Finally the cab pulled in front of Saks red awning, and the doorman greeted her mother by name. Clarice smiled politely, handed him a generous tip, and they made their way through the olfactory factory of the perfume counters and then to the elegant wooden elevators at the back.

"Why don't you come with me to Palm Springs for the week?" suggested her mother as the elevator started to rise.

Edie considered it for a second but her idea of a vacation didn't involve five-hundred-calorie diets, or four-hour yoga sessions. Edie believed in five-hundred-calorie desserts, and baking in the sun, and hunky cabana boys by the name of Jose.

Or Tyler.

A momentary picture of a sun-drenched Tyler overwhelmed her brain. A flash of Tyler dribbling suntan oil on her bare skin—now that was a vacation, she thought with a secret smile. "Sorry, Mom, got a hot date."

Her mother managed to restrain her curiosity until they were seated, until all packages were tucked away under the white-draped tables, until her mother removed her sunglasses and could stare at Edie with the necessary intent. "A hot date with whom?"

At first Edie considered not saying anything about Tyler, but it was her mother's anniversary, and she knew that Tyler would make her mother happy. Not that it meant anything, and she needed to make her mother understand that…before she got her hopes up. "I don't think you'd like him. He's a history buff, high education, low-income potential, visiting from out of state, and he's on the rebound after a really hideous breakup. I'm just trying to help out a friend, get him over the rough spots and then back on his feet."

"Your father's fundraiser is scheduled for next month.

I suppose you've forgotten. You could bring your new friend."

"I don't think he's the gala type, Mom. Sorry."

"But you'll be there? I could use the moral support."

Edie stared at her mother, slack-jawed, accompanied by skeptical eyes. "You need me like Seattle needs rain."

"Poke fun all you want, but I was being serious. Besides, Dr. Hardy's wife always brags on her daughter and the precious grandchildren and how they all went together on a cruise to the Bahamas for Christmas. Sometimes I just want to tell her to stick it up her perfectly sculpted ass. Sometimes I just want to show you off."

Sometimes her mother chose to color outside the lines of reality, too. It was endearing, yet also not very smart. "I'm not very show-off-worthy," stated Edie, who was meticulously neat about her reality lines. It avoided many problems in her life.

"That's not true. You clean up very well, and although you don't have to bring a date, you could bring a date...."

"Maybe you could be my date, Mom. Or, we could really shock Dad and rent a couple of escorts for the evening. Young, studly and hanging on our every word."

Her mother laughed and Edie felt herself warm just a little bit. They ordered lunch—Clarice: cobb salad, Edie: double-fudge brownie. As they ate, Edie watched as the weekend shopping elite relieved their feet, their pallets and their wallets, all in one fell swoop. Alternatively, her mother waved at friends, chatted about gardening and looked completely at home.

Edie listened attentively, as any good daughter should, but amidst the subdued elegance, her tank top felt a little too tacky and the streak in her hair—today's color: cerulean blue—seemed more conspicuous than she normally liked. Every now and again, her mother, sensing Edie's discomfort, would pat her hand, which didn't do diddly for the discomfortness, but it did make her love her mother even more for trying.

Eventually the plates were cleared, all that was left were the last drops of Veuve Clicquot Brut Yellow Label. Also remaining was her mother's need to torture her daughter into social conformity. All in all, it was a good strategy for her mom, worthy of the CIA, as she'd peppered the conversation with perfectly timed glances of quiet suffering.

"Bring your date to the gala," her mother repeated, but Edie, not so unsuspecting, shook her head.

"Don't think so, Mom. Picture this—you very charmingly interrogate him. And then we have Dad, who will ask him why he's not saving lives on a daily basis. After a bad dinner with rubberized chicken, all the surgeons will commence their back-slapping ritual, telling great stories in ten-syllable words that absolutely no one can understand. Good times. *Not.*"

Her mother, who much like Edie did not take well to rejection, smiled magnificently, which was a clue to her true displeasure. "I'm sure your father would be very nice to whomever you chose to bring."

"It's not that big of a deal, Mom. Tyler's just one of many. You know me." Edie smiled, equally magnificently, which loosely translated to Hell Will Freeze First.

Her mother, much more willing to live with rejection than Edie, sighed and looked at her daughter with long-suffering blue eyes. Finally, recognizing the futility of transforming her daughter into anything other than Edie, Clarice dabbed at her mouth with the cloth napkin.

"Don't let yourself get hurt," she advised, sticking to a mother-daughter script handed down through generations.

"Don't worry, Mom. I'm smart." *Smarter than you,* she thought to herself.

"Yes, you are, Edie. You're smart, beautiful and you

always sell yourself short," lectured the woman who spent every wedding anniversary solo.

Edie leaned in close. "Can I let you in on a secret, Mom?"

"I live for your tidbits of personal advice."

Edie took a sip of champagne, letting the bubbles tickle her nose, and then met her mother's eyes. "If you set the bar low, you'll never be disappointed." Perhaps there was a hint of wistfulness in her own eyes that was not quite obscured by the effervescence of champagne.

Then, the woman who had loved and nurtured Edie for twenty-eight years raised her glass. Her diamond rings were blinding in the dazzling light. The glare was almost enough to obscure the wistfulness in her mother's eyes, but Edie knew better. She had learned long ago to look past the shimmering, pretty things that hypnotized the rest of the world.

At her daughter's look of sympathy, Clarice took a sip of champagne and smiled because the Higgins women both loved their bubbles. "One day that bar's going to be so low that it'll hit you in the head, knock you out and you'll suffer from amnesia, forgetting all your bad intentions, and instead end up married to a stable, respectable man with a wonderful job, high community standing, who loves you exactly as you deserve. Before you know it, you'll end up pregnant, and then, when your hormones are raging, and your ankles are swelling, I will look at you and say, 'Ha!'"

Edie laughed and lifted her glass. "To hell."

Her mother smiled serenely. "Amen."

7

SATURDAY WAS TYLER'S first day under the rheumy scrutiny of Dr. Herbert Edwards, M.D., FACS, Ph.D, and it was exhilarating. Videos of surgeries were never fun, but there was an energy in the room, an excitement. The brain power in the room was the best of the best, and focused on one thing: mastering the organ at the very top of the body's food chain—*the heart*.

And the ACT/Keating Endowment Award, he reminded himself. It was the pot of cardiac gold that sat at the end of the rainbow, the meritorious achievement that told the world that there was no better cardiacthoracic surgeon. And it wasn't given for golf scores.

The large auditorium was packed with medical types who had shown up for the weekend kickoff. There were doctors, interns and even a few administrators. From the podium on the stage, Dr. Edwards was showing a video of his latest technique in endovascular stent grafting, while explaining how the aortic surgical program would guide his fellow professionals into the new world of advanced medical technologies.

It was career-altering, the future of cardio-technology, and Tyler would be a part of it all. The intern next to him noticed the smile on his face, and Tyler nodded toward the stage. "Takes me back to this one time when I had a descending thoracic aortic aneurysm. Eighteen hours of surgery that nearly got the better of me but the guy lived, went home in less than a week and he's now diving off the Caymans, and sends me a card every year at Christmas."

"Wicked awesome," replied the twenty-four-year-old resident who was still green enough to believe that eighteen hours of surgery was a good thing.

The purpose of the fellowship was to find new, non-invasive methods that were of less risk to the patient. No more digging into chest cavities. Yes, it was healthier for the patient, but deep in the heart of every surgeon was the thrill of cutting into skin, and then mastering the miracle that was the human heart.

While Dr. Edwards explained the long-term benefits of a homograft valve, Tyler wondered about the other aspect of the human heart—the other, less fascinating, and more irrational part. The things that women expected from men.

The emotional crap.

Was that why Cynthia had cheated? Was he truly responsible? Was he cold? A brick? The more he thought about this, the more his head began to ache and he wondered if women were responsible for intracranial aneurysm. Probably. He pressed his fingers to his temples and then he moved his wayward thoughts from the crisis of understanding the female psyche, to the more pleasing idea of straddling the female body.

God, he was turning into a lech.

After the presentation was over, he called Edie to find out where the first lesson would be. Maybe she hadn't been serious, but the more he thought about it, the more he decided that if he did have a problem, then he wanted to fix it.

"We don't need to do that," Edie explained, and he

planted himself on a nearby couch because apparently this was not going to be a short conversation.

"I think it would help."

"You're trying to humor me. You don't have to."

Tyler remained silent, trying to determine what he should say. "No, I think we should. I have a problem."

It was the perfect choice of words. "You don't," she told him, which was nice to hear, but Tyler had now decided that he needed to go through the steps and discover if there was something missing within him. And then once he knew, he could fix it. Like surgery. Only more difficult.

"I think I do. Cynthia said..." he began, then trailed off in a depressed manner.

"Oh." Edie's voice was quiet, reflective, believing. "You're right. I'd forgotten."

Tyler smiled to himself. Mission accomplished.

She told him where to meet, and he hung up.

Piece of cake.

That night he met Edie at exactly eight o'clock at a card shop on Prince Street. Why a card shop Tyler wasn't sure, but Edie seemed enthusiastic, although when it came to helping people in need, he suspected that Edie would never be unenthusiastic.

The shop was tiny. There were four rows of cards, three shelves of useless animal statues in pastel colors and two rows of incense, samples of which were now burning and stinking up the place. In spite of all that negativity, he found himself smiling as Edie approached.

Tonight she was wearing an outrageously short yellow skirt that showed off long, tan legs, a green T-shirt that hugged her breasts and neon pink sandals topped with small plastic pink flamingos that he wouldn't normally consider sexy, but somehow, when Edie wore them, his eager cock thought it was the hottest thing ever.

Go figure.

At the beginning, there was that one awkward moment when a man who had previously engaged in wild monkey sex with said female was now supposed to have polite, friendly conversation and forget that he knew her body intimately, or that she had sucked him until…

These sorts of moments were new to Tyler, who previously had thought wild monkey sex was beneath him. Soon his brain resumed functioning, his heart rate calmed.

Acting as if she hadn't noticed the awkwardness, Edie casually strolled over to the display racks, removed a card and then waved it under his eyes. "This is a greeting card. The card was invented over a thousand years ago as an expression of a man's feelings for a woman, because yes, even in the Dark Ages, men could not express their thoughts. But as a historian, you would know that."

Tyler blinked before he realized that he was supposed to be a historian. "My specialty is ancient medicine, not textiles," he said quickly.

"Ancient medicine, like ritualistic sacrifices to the gods?"

"More like what the Egyptians did with the brain and the heart," he hedged, racking his brain to remember what the Egyptians did with the brain and the heart.

"Oh, yeah, where they removed the brain tissue through the nose? Frankly, I thought their surgical skills were way off, but how they used honey to treat infections? Who'd have ever thought of that?"

Tyler nodded sagely. "It was ingenious, but let's get back to greeting cards."

"You're right, but you'll have to tell me about the mummification process. I think it's fascinating. I had a class…" She closed her eyes, then opened them again. "Back to greeting cards. So, eventually, the process was streamlined, commercialized and outsourced to create mass-produced, assembly-line type products that are supposed to express our deepest emotional connections to other human beings. It's not pretty. It is a slap in the face to a romantic female, and yet...there is value and education there. People read into the gesture. Women love the gestures. Remember that."

Disdainfully, she picked up a bright pink card with a pansy on the front, held it between her thumb and forefinger and began to read aloud. "'No woman compares to the flower that is you.'"

Tyler only partially suppressed the gagging sound that he assumed was the appropriate response, but Edie was merciless. "It is trite. It is meaningless. It says 'I don't know what I love about you, so I shall compare you to an object that we have genetically Frankensteined until all fragrance and uniqueness has been cultivated out.'"

"And that's bad," guessed Tyler.

"Not all men are as perceptive as you. See you're learning what women want in men."

"And that's why I'm here. To learn from the best."

And it had nothing to do with the feel of your legs wrapped around my waist. Nothing at all. Would she wear the sandals with pink flamingos when they had sex? If they had sex, he corrected. *If. If* they did have sex, he wanted her to leave the flamingos on.

Pervert.

Not guessing the sordid train of his thoughts, Edie smiled encouragingly. "Exactly. But the key here is to analyze the woman in question."

"Who?" Tyler asked, because he didn't think they were talking about Edie, but in his experience, women liked it when the discussion revolved around themselves rather than another female.

"I don't know. We're talking hypotheticals, and we have to pretend," answered Edie, with a get-with-the-program look that didn't bode well for future sex. "Create a woman.

So what in the relationship makes her special and unique above all women?"

"She's great-looking."

Edie shrugged. "It's not a good idea to start with the physical. Start instead with her personality, her mind, her heart."

Tyler frowned because every human being had the same ten ounces of tissue and muscle that constructed the heart. Yes, some epicardiums were thinner than others, some chordae tendineae were stretched so far that valve function was compromised, and some arteries got so clogged they needed to be grafted with something that had a little more kick. But he didn't think Edie would appreciate knowing all this. In fact, he suspected that if he tried to educate her on the anatomical workings of the human heart, he would be demonstrating the very shortcomings of his heart that she was trying to repair.

Edie Higgins, a heart surgeon in a metaphorical sense.

The pink flamingos began to tap on the floor.

"She'd be very witty," he replied, which he thought would prove that he wasn't completely hopeless.

"No, no, no," she said, pushing at the short strands of her hair, acting with all the impatience of every great surgeon he'd ever known. Apparently "witty" wasn't the answer she wanted. "Dig deeper, Tyler. What about this imaginary woman makes you happy? Do you get happy when she smiles at you? Does she ease your burden or calm the stormy tides of your day-to-day grind?"

Tyler considered the question and realized that no woman had never eased his burden, because he didn't have a burden that needed easing, so it probably wasn't germane. Unless Edie considered a hard-on a burden to be eased? Nope, he decided. Definitely not greeting-card material.

"She's not a 'stormy tides' sort of female," he said, and Edie returned the card to the display rack.

"All right. Let's go back to the simple stuff. Why did you pick this woman and ask her out?"

Tyler tracked back to his relationship with Cynthia and remembered that he'd been set up by Paul, his roommate during his residency, who was trying to get Cynthia's friend into bed, but only had two hours for social activities because his surgical rotation was killing him, and college women never bought that excuse, so Paul had assumed that Tyler could do some of the heavy lifting for him.

Why did women even fall for men? If Tyler were a woman, he'd be a lesbian because he wouldn't want to date a man because frankly, all men were pigs.

Realizing that he was going to have to be inventive, Tyler finally came up with an answer that he knew would make Edie happy. "She had a nice laugh."

Edie laughed, and he beamed proudly. "And now we're talking! What made her laugh?"

Tyler blinked, thinking again. The most likely cause was the Long Island ice teas. That night he'd ended up walking Cynthia home from the bar, tucking her into bed and leaving two aspirin on her nightstand. Cynthia had thought it was romantic, even after Tyler had explained the bonding properties of acetylsalicylic acid, and how ASA suppresses the production of prostaglandins, which are the key pain-transmitters to the brain, thus eliminating…

Edie was clearly waiting for his answer, expecting some new breakthrough in his sensitivity training. Tyler wanted her to feel as if he had actually had a breakthrough and then inspiration struck. Cynthia had always loved it when he confessed his flaws. He could be imperfect.

"I made a joke about something. I'm not very good at jokes."

Edie touched his arm, an encouraging gesture not de-signed to send further blood to his cock.

Off-topic, Tyler.

"So when she laughed, it made you happy, and made you feel good about yourself."

Perhaps, but Cynthia's laugh had never made him happy, especially that first night, because Cynthia had been laughing at pretty much everything. Actually, it was *in spite of* the constant laughter that Tyler had liked her, liked her nondemanding personality, and when he'd called the next day to see if she had recovered, things had progressed from there.

Not romantic. *Practical.*

Edie was studying him, her impatient brown eyes urging him to make some forward progress away from the apparently evil side of practicality. Wanting to make Edie happy, he decided to steer the conversation in another direction completely. About her. "People like to feel good about themselves, don't they? What makes you happy?" he asked, oh, so cleverly.

She glanced at the cards and worried her lower lip. "I like to help people," she admitted, as if it was some secret that he couldn't have guessed.

Like driving the cab for Barnaby, he thought, and then was shocked to hear the words aloud.

"And helping you," she added. A woman brushed by them in the aisle, and Edie smiled at her, getting a smile in return. She did that to people, dazzled them with her buoyancy, confusing them, befuddling them, and then dragging them into the pink flamingo world that she had created.

And most dangerous of all, she made them *want* to be there.

With the pink flamingos.

Having sex.

His intentions were good, honorable, yet here he was,

standing with her in a card shop, trying to pay attention, but knowing this was something he was never going to comprehend, all the while his randy subconscious had already stripped her naked, and had her legs on his shoulders, and her breasts in his mouth.

And didn't she know all that?

Edie stared at him, not so whimsical anymore, her eyes had darkened and her smile fell to something more comprehending.

Yes, she did know all that because Edie Higgins was many things. Unfortunately, stupid was not one of them.

"Let's phone a friend."

"Now?" he asked, glancing at the narrow aisles, the wretched Saturday-night card shoppers, and the monkey bookends that grinned at him from their perch above the stacks.

"Yeah. You're going to have a real, honest conversation with another woman." She pulled a notebook and pen out of her Save a Plant, Kill a Vegan bookbag, and started to write. "I'll get you started on what to say, you improvise, and then we'll do a postmortem after you're done."

In Tyler's line of work, postmortem was never a good experience. "Do we have to do that?"

"It's the best way to learn."

Well, yes, but the patient was dead, so ergo, Tyler had failed. However, Edie didn't realize that Tyler didn't like dwelling on his shortcomings, and she seemed to like dwelling on his shortcomings, and frankly, if they were going to talk about his shortcomings, he was glad they were confined to a simple phone conversation. "Okay," he agreed.

"Who am I supposed to call?"

"Do you remember Passion from the other night?"

"She was one of the dancers," Tyler guessed.

"Exactly," she responded, beaming.

"Why are we doing this?"

"Practice."

He didn't need practice.

"How are you going to start?"

"Hello?"

"That's good," she told him. "And then?"

And then things got muddier. "How are you?" he said.

"Nah. Don't ask how she's doing. Then the conversation gets bogged down into the minute-by-minute minutiae of the day, and you want to avoid that. Instead, surprise her."

"How do I do that?"

"Ask her something unexpected, or tell her something unexpected. Tell her that you saw a woman on the street, and she reminded you of her."

"I should lie?"

"It's not a lie," Edie assured him. Edie, who was not party to the pigginess that inhabited the male brain.

Med school had been so much easier.

"I didn't see a lot of women today," he said.

"Okay, let's find something else." Her eyes scanned the cards in front of her and then she grabbed one from the stack. "How about 'I was thinking about you.'"

Stubbornly Tyler shook his head, unwilling to compromise his values any further, and also because he wanted to ditch all the emotional hoodoo and discover if Edie was wearing a bra.

It was at that moment, as Tyler was remembering the exact color of Edie's nipples, that she handed him a piece of paper. "All right. Here's her number. Go ahead and call and just go with what you feel."

Go with what you feel? Oh, God. It was hell. This was hell.

Unfortunately, Edie looked so innocent, as if he was capable of emotional hoodoo, and he didn't want her to think that. Or that he was an emotional coward. He could do this. He could.

It was easy.

Determined to overcome such shortcomings, Tyler got out his phone and dialed.

"Hello."

"Tyler?"

"Hi, Passion."

"Tyler, this is Austen. Your brother."

"I know. This is Tyler. I wanted to call and hear your voice," he told his brother while grinning happily at Edie.

He was a pig.

"Why are you calling me and why are you calling me Passion? Who is Passion?"

"It was a long day today," Tyler started, and then noticed Edie shaking her head in warning. Minutiae. That was minutiae. God forgive him, he was a relationship failure.

"Is there a woman there? Are you trying to shake her? Faking the call back home? I don't even do that, Tyler. Are you drunk?"

"I was just thinking how great you looked."

"Tyler, men don't talk to people this way. Are you being mugged? Is this some freaky code that I'm supposed to understand? Let me know if I need to call 911."

While Austen was spiraling into a panic, Edie was scribbling in her notebook. She shot him a dark look and then showed him the page.

You might as well tell her she's a genetically neutered pansy.

If a greeting card could be stabbed between one's own eyes, Tyler would have done it.

8

THERE WAS SOMETHING SWEET about watching Tyler sweat through this conversation. The store's customers continued to shove past him, shooting him their pushy New Yorker looks.

Edie knew this wasn't his natural state, but he didn't complain, didn't whine. No, he was plodding through the twelve steps of courtship hell in order to make her happy.

In order to get laid, an insidious voice corrected her.

Did that make her a bad person that she was enjoying his torture? Possibly, but in between the twitchy frowns, he would watch her steadily, *knowingly,* and Edie had the acute feeling that Tyler Hart was aware of what Edie was doing. Such really smart awareness tickled her in sexual places. Mind games, that's what they called it. If she spent a lot of time analyzing her prior relationships, which Edie didn't, she might have noted that most of them were with dim bulbs, men who were a few tokens short of a full fare, but Tyler was different. Tyler was smart, and this whole undercurrent of crazy tension kept her senses tingling and alive.

Mind games could be fun.

At first.

While she watched him talk on the phone, he watched her listen, and his conversation grew even more uncomfortable, and not so much fun. After each robotic interchange, his twitchy frowns grew even more twitchy, until at last, she was ready to pull the plug. Needing to look somewhere else, she stared down at the berber carpet.

"I can't do this," Tyler said to someone, and whether it was Passion or Edie, she didn't know. Her head shot up, meeting his eyes.

"Of course you can," Edie whispered urgently, and she could feel a twitchy frown of her own. Seeing the intent look in those undim eyes, she suspected he was about to do something to mess with Edie's status quo, and Edie was desperately fond of her status quo.

"I'm talking to my brother. Not Passion," he told her.

Edie's frown grew even twitchier, even as she could hear the shouts emerging from his phone: "No, Tyler, *no!*"

A man with an overpowering cologne and too much hair product brushed past her to peruse the graduation cards. Tyler edged away from Graduation and into Thinking of You.

Seeing no choice, Edie followed.

Smartly ignoring the warnings from his brother and stupidly ignoring her growing panic, Tyler stuffed his phone in his pocket and everyone's twitchy frowns stopped. On his face there was something new and even more dangerous. Resoluteness. Firm resolve, and the little hearts and flower cards beckoned behind them.

"I didn't feel right about talking to another woman."

"In front of me? I can respect that. I didn't mean to encroach on your personal space. I do that a lot, jumping into situations that really don't concern me, and usually people don't mind, because usually I can fix things—"

"Edie," he interrupted.

"What?"

"It has nothing to do with privacy."

"Oh. Well, you struck me as a very private person, and I thought—"

"Edie."

"Yes?"

"That's not it."

"What is it?" she asked, not liking his guessing game, not liking the hearts and flowers showcased behind him, not liking the whole dangerous trend of this conversation.

"Do you have to ask?" he said, raising one supercilious brow at her, which normally would have ticked her off, but now it only scared her. She didn't need to ask why because Tyler Hart wouldn't do rascally things like flirt with another woman in front of her, even though she told him to, and she wished he were a little more squeevy so that she didn't have to…

Respect him so much.

Everything would be a lot easier if he were like all the other guys who had to use meaningless lines, or mooch her for a few bucks, or drank too much in order to ditch responsibility at the door. But Tyler didn't do anything of those things. Not. One.

No, he had to be *honest*.

He wanted her, she reminded herself. That was the Why of all these actions.

He was no different than any other male.

And why was her brain not okay with his honesty thing?

What was the big deal? It *was* a big freaking deal, that's what it was, because the Tylers of the world were upstanding, good-hearted. They didn't tell lies…comfortably. They were the very sort of men her parents would approve of.

Damn. It.

"Do you want a drink?" asked Dudley Do-Right.

"Are you trying to get me drunk?" she asked hopefully.

"No." More of that honesty thing. Edie struggled to push her hair behind her ear. Tyler reached out and did it for her, and it wasn't a sexy, come-hither touch. It was a comfortable touch, an easy touch, and Edie could feel the panic welling in her stomach, pushing up through her throat. "I don't do relationships," she stated, firmly meeting his gaze.

"You've said that many times."

"Sex is it," she affirmed.

"Yes, you've said that, as well." The perky salesclerk started flirting with Mr. Cologne, and exchanging meaningless lines, and Edie considered edging closer to that conversation, because frankly, it was easier. But Tyler, perhaps sensing her extreme uneasiness, perhaps due to the nervous tic in her eye, picked up a pink card and examined it with more attention than the damned thing deserved. "'You make everything sweeter.' What's wrong with that?"

And now they were back in her comfort zone, critiquing overwrought sentimentality. "Oh, come on. Do you really have to ask? What is sweeter? Sweeter than what? Good grief, too much sugar makes people throw up."

"Actually, it's more intolerance or malabsorption. Fructose can in fact be used as an antiemetic."

"Then that's what's wrong with it."

"Have you ever sent a greeting card to anyone?" he asked casually, carelessly.

"My father," she said casually, carelessly.

Tyler didn't look at her, instead he studied the stacks of cards in front of him and began randomly picking some out. Edie wasn't sure why he was overindulging in greeting cards, but they weren't talking, and her eye tic wasn't bothering her anymore, so she played along.

Apparently Tyler wasn't a meticulous shopper, because

he had a stack of about thirty cards when he approached the clerk and asked to pay.

After that, they walked out into the night, and headed for a bar in the next block. Secretly, Edie approved. Sure, he had a year's supply of greeting cards, but if she were lucky, they were going to order a few shots, and critique the hell out of all of them.

His phone rang and he looked at the display and then swore.

Instantly, Edie was on alert. "Cynthia?"

He shook his head, pressed the button to ignore. "No." He pulled open the bar's heavy wooden door, and she followed him inside.

It was an old-style place with wooden floors and three long mahogany counters that outlined the packed room. Behind the bar, there were photographs of average Joes who likely frequented the place. In less than a second, Tyler had found a newly vacated table.

"How did you know they were going to leave?" asked Edie. She hadn't seen any of the usual signs: empty drink glasses, rolled-up napkins, or a leather folio with the bill.

Tyler shrugged. "I gave them a fifty."

"Very creative. You don't usually see that much imagination from out-of-towners."

"I don't like to wait," he explained, sitting down at the table, and laying out the greeting cards in front of him. A waitress introduced herself as Tessa and took their drink orders. Tyler asked for a diet soda. Edie asked for tequila. He looked at her expectantly, and slowly, reluctantly, she changed it to soda. "With lots of ice, please," she added, lest he think that she was one of those lemming sort of women who needed a man to tell them what to do.

While she sipped her soda, which was mostly ice, she watched as he studied the cards, then pulled a Swiss Army knife from his jacket pocket and began to cut.

At first she assumed it was random mutilation, and there was a second when she worried that she was now sharing drinks with a very nice, very polite sociopath, but then an order began to emerge, ransom-note style:

I LIKE YOU.

Surprisingly enough, the words did not make her feel nervous. Perhaps it was the cacophony of curlicue fonts and sugary colors, which sort of overwhelmed the message. Or maybe it was because he was ignoring her, concentrating on his work. Apparently, Tyler had more cards to destroy.

As the pile of paper letters began to grow, she noticed the confidence in how he worked, the edges remarkably neat, which was no shocker because he probably handled precise edges every day at the museum. In fact, she liked his graceful movements, watching the way his fingers displayed an easy efficiency. Very few men had such talented hands.

A few minutes later, those very deft hands laid out the second message on the table.

I LIKE YOUR PINK BIRDS.

A woman at the next table glanced at the words, and raised a disapproving brow. Edie flashed her sandals at the woman, who looked away, now suitably shamed, which was a good thing because the third message was much more lurid.

I DREAMED OF SEEING YOU NAKED. AGAIN.

Unable to stop herself, Edie began to giggle. "Creative. Sort of like ancient Sanskrit."

"I didn't want to draw pictures," Tyler explained, shrug-

ging in that manly way of men who know they're doing
good, but don't want to act as if they were expecting such
good acts to be noticed, even though they secretly were.
It wasn't a gesture Edie saw very often in New York, but
she recognized it from the movies.

"I studied Sanskrit when I was a junior," she told him.
"They were pretty graphic back then."

"Yeah," he said, and then he leaned over and he kissed
her, and it wasn't a graphic kiss, it was short, soft and designed to burrow into places that Edie didn't like men to
burrow to, but Edie found herself kissing him back. Short,
soft, as if she were now considering said burrowing, but
before she could commit to further madness, her phone
rang. Thankfully, regrettably, she answered it and then
promptly swore, partly because of the cause of the inter-
ruption, and partly because she was more shaken from the
kiss than she wanted to admit.

While she listened to the conversation on the other end,
Tyler looked at her, not completely surprised. Finally, she
hung up.

"It's work," she explained.

"Work?" he asked casually, sipping his diet soda and
looking completely unshaken.

"The diner," she answered, sipping her ice. But right
now, she needed a distraction, and the drink was all she
had.

He leaned back and studied her. "You work at the
diner?"

Edie waited a beat, hesitated, glanced down at the evis-
cerated greeting cards and decided to tell the truth. "I own
the diner."

"You don't act like the owner."

"How is an owner supposed to act?" she asked, somewhat defensively, because, she had just told him a rather

large secret, and he didn't have to go all third degree about it. Honestly, it was no big deal. No big deal at all.

"Why be all hush-hush about it?"

"I'm not one of those people who needs to toot her own horn," she said.

"Why not? If you've done something to be proud of, why not share?"

"Spoken like a typical man." The tone of her voice could be construed as insulting if one wanted to think that.

"That's very sexist," he shot back in what could be construed as an insulting tone if one wanted to think that. Edie did.

"I don't need somebody's approval for my actions, or my choices in life. I prefer to live without it."

"That's very nihilistic of you," he offered as way of explanation. She liked his comment better than saying, "You don't want your father to approve, and so, you live your life with a very stick-in-the-eye approach because you're stubborn, and don't want him to think that he's right."

Although she knew Tyler didn't know about her stick-in-the-eye life-attitude, she knew he knew that whatever her reason, it wasn't exactly healthy, and so she was quite pleased at his gracious or even—dare she say it—chivalrous behavior.

And it didn't even make her twitch.

"There's a slight emergency," she told him, but before she could explain further, he laid some bills on the table, and they were at the curb climbing into a cab.

Everything he did was handled with that sort of quiet authority, and she stayed silent as they rode the ten blocks down Forty-Ninth Street to her diner.

The booths were nearly full, an eclectic Saturday night mix of young party-goers, older couples avoiding the bigger restaurant crowds and a few singletons with their newspapers and cups of coffee.

Khandi, the night manager, greeted Edie with a weary shake of the head. Patience's emergencies were somewhat of a regular occurrence, and Khandi had little patience for Patience.

Once they made it to the bustling kitchen, Edie heard the source of the problem soon enough.

Patience was huddled over the sink, sobbing with all the pain of a woman who had just had her heart broken. Edie knew that Patience got her heart broken on a monthly basis, but the waitress seemed to always develop heartbreak-amnesia and trusted far more easily than she should.

That, and her taste in men showcased somewhere below reptilian.

Keeping her judgments to herself, Edie grabbed a handful of paper towels from the dispenser, walked over to Patience and hugged her tight, because even stupid women didn't deserve to get hurt.

"He's not worth it," she whispered, dabbing at the spots where Patience's mascara had started to run, all the while mentally condemning the men who had no idea of the damage they could cause.

"I know."

"You'll find somebody better," Edie reassured her, grabbing a cloth napkin and running it under the warm water.

"I don't think so," Patience sniffed. "What man is going to want me?"

"A very smart one. Look, they're already lining up." Edie turned and nodded to where Tyler stood, his back to the grill, looking so much better than a reptile, and Edie felt a rock in her throat.

"Who are you?" asked Patience, curious about the presence of a man in the kitchen. Usually men weren't allowed in the back of the diner, except for Ira, who was over seventy. If Tyler noticed Edie's discriminatory practice, he didn't let on.

"Edie's latest victim," he answered without hesitation. Right then, Stella, the cook, flipped some pastrami on the sizzling surface of the grill, sending drops popping in all directions. Cautiously, Tyler moved away.

Patience started to laugh, and even cracked a smile at Tyler, who was wearing his uncomfortable frown, but his eyes were nice. Edie met those warm eyes and smiled at him herself.

"You're not going to take her to a strip club, are you?" he asked, while Patience washed her face with the warm rag.

"No, someplace better." Edie cocked her head toward her approaching manager. "Khandi, raid the bottom drawer in the office. There's a little black Armani in there that would look great."

"I can't wear my Converse with that," Patience protested, whose fashion sense wasn't nearly as promiscuous as Edie's.

Edie took a look at the red high-tops in question. "Of course you can." She nudged Tyler in the ribs, awaiting confirmation.

"It's a nice look," Tyler added without hesitation.

Khandi nodded, as well. "Go with it. Can't say the old look has gotten you far."

Eventually, Patience agreed and Khandi went for the dress. Every now and then Patience would glance curiously at Tyler, but she was too nonconfrontational to say anything, unlike Stella, the thrice-retired school teacher who lived to make trouble.

"What's wrong with *him?*" Stella asked, slapping a sandwich together and adding a pickle to the plate, before sliding it down the counter and ringing the bell with a lot of pent-up aggression.

"Nothing's wrong with him," replied Edie, who saw

Tyler's perfection as an actual flaw, but she wasn't about to explain that in front of heartbroken Patience.

"There's something wrong with everyone that Edie's with." Patience politely acknowledged what Tyler had said earlier about himself.

"I'm in an emotional coma," Tyler explained. "She's trying to bring me back to life."

"Should have known," said Stella, now satisfied that Tyler was no more than the usual.

Edie suppressed a sigh of relief. Emotional coma, she thought, eying Tyler thoughtfully. *You know, that might work.*

While Patience was changing in the bathroom, Edie headed for the office to check Sunday morning's delivery order. Tyler didn't say a word, watching intently as Edie relaxed in her desk chair as if she owned it. Which she did, she reminded herself, flipping through the various invoices.

After verifying that yes, there would be food for the following week, Edie shot him a fast look. "Emotional coma. That's pretty good."

"My brother tells me that all the time." Tyler assessed the small space, but didn't judge, which was much more courteous than Edie would have been. She supposed that was one of the differences between Texas and New York. New Yorkers knew better than to care.

"He sounds a lot livelier than you," Edie told him, a slight verbal jab only because she wished he weren't so nice, so likeable, and thought a few purposely chosen words might raise some hackles.

"He is," he confirmed, hackles completely unraised.

"Hmmm," she murmured, fixing her eyes on the antique fixtures, running numbers in her head, because her office had never seemed so tiny, so ramshackle, and even though she knew he wasn't judging, she was making judgments for him, and Edie never liked to be judged.

He let her sit there, mentally fidgeting, until she finally—courageously—lifted her eyes from the boxes and papers and numbers and contemplated the source of her anxiety.

What was it about him that scared her so much? She'd stared down muggers, haggled with bank managers, threatened Con Ed with legal hari-kari if they shut down Stella's power. Tyler Hart shouldn't even make her blink. But he did. Was it the thoughtful dark eyes, the nose that was just an inch on the wrong side of arrogant, or the serious mouth that he kept firmly shut? His wasn't a face for the magazines or the movies, he was too reserved for business, but sometimes she could see further than she wanted. He gave away nothing, no clue, no gesture, but her mind recognized things in him.

There were people in the world who climbed in the boxing ring that was life, people who opened themselves up to the world, taking punches and reaping the big gold trophies for the pain. And then there were the others. The ones who hid. Sometimes they hid behind a big mouth and a lot of manufactured bravado, and sometimes they hid behind a serious mouth and thoughtful dark eyes. In the end, though, no matter how you did it, hidden was hidden.

Edie knew why she kept herself out of the ring. But why Tyler?

"What are you going to do, now?" Tyler asked, which on the surface was such an innocent question that Edie, taking the surface answer, shot him a grin.

"Right now, we bowl." The serious mouth didn't move, but she noticed the flicker of disappointment in his eyes. Edie pushed away from the chair, and closed the book on the diner. Disappointment didn't bother her. Never had.

Twenty minutes later, the mismatched threesome arrived

at the lanes at Chelsea Pier, an intriguing mix of dim cock-tail lounge, party lights in shades of blue, purple and pink, loud, throbbing music, high-backed leather couches and bowling lanes. The place was packed full of men. Old men, young men, bowling teams in their coordinating uniforms and a small group of teenagers who were blasting lasers in the arcade. Amidst all that testosterone and blaring rock music, Patience looked ready to bolt.

Tentatively Patience entered, her hair neatly styled, the Armani clinging exactly as Edie'd known it would. When she wasn't wearing a yellow apron, Patience could be quite the looker, and heads turned as she passed.

Directly in front of them, a teenager type manned the long black shelves that were packed with shiny balls and shoes. Everything was artfully arranged, completely unlike any other bowling alley in the world—which was the main reason for the place's popularity.

Tyler stared impassively at his red, white and blue shoes, but when he looked at Edie, all he did was quirk a brow.

"Scared?" she taunted.

"Nope," Tyler answered. "You?"

"Of ugly shoes?" Edie scoffed. "Ha. Nothing like bowl-ing shoes to reveal the lily-livered cowards among us."

Realizing they were one missing, Edie noted that Pa-tience was now frozen in place, a vision in high-tops and Armani. It took a strong woman to carry off the look, and before the night was over, Edie was determined that Patience would be transformed.

Edie stared at her, humming "Ride of the Valkyries." "I can't bowl," Patience protested, but before she could wimp out, Edie thrust a pair of bowling shoes into her hand.

"Neither can I. That's what makes it fun."

THE CLOCK ON THE neon display overhead said 3:00 a.m., but Tyler didn't need sleep. He didn't need caffeine. Instead, he had the immense pleasure of watching Edie bowl, or try to. When it was her turn, she'd bend over and push the ball down the lane. The technique was completely lacking in skill, but Tyler wasn't concerned, because when she bent over—if a man were so desperate as to lean low in his seat—the very edges of what looked to be blue polka-dot panties were exposed. Sure, it was the horniest man who thought blue polka-dots were sexy, but Tyler was well and truly seduced.

Midway through the second game, Patience found two other ladies who were also there to pick up men and shortly, the three of them were seated in the bar, ordering froufrou coffees and discussing the latest Nicholas Sparks novel. Tyler wasn't sure who Nicholas Sparks was, but Patience seemed to be a fan, even though she said, "Somebody always dies." Tyler considered enquiring further, but then it was Edie's turn to bowl again. When a man had to pick between five-hanky novels and the finer details of a woman's underwear, books were for the birds.

"You didn't bring her here to pick up a guy?" Tyler asked, as Edie watched her ball drift helplessly into the gutter. Most red-blooded competitors would be discouraged, but Edie bowled with that same sort of kamikaze attitude that she did everything else, and didn't seem to mind at all.

She turned to him, hands on curvy hips, and shook her head. "Nah. It's too soon. You know what becomes of the broken-hearted? They go out bowling. Every Saturday night there's a huge group of the dateless here."

He glanced over to where Patience was sitting, eating and laughing as if she hadn't been contorted with misery earlier. "She's going to be okay?"

"Until tomorrow night, when she's alone. And then she'll call."

When her score flashed on the video overhead, Edie

murmured something obscene. Tyler walked up behind her, not wanting to gloat, but yes, there was an extra bounce in his step. His first throws had gone in the gutter, but once he realized that he was hooking right, he'd managed to compensate, and now he was beating Edie's ass, not that it was a monumental accomplishment, but he suspected Edie was far too accustomed to losing. Although, to be fair, some of her poor choices accounted for her issues with success, or lack thereof. However, since technically it was those very same poor choices that had put her in his bed, he didn't think he needed to point that out.

Bowling hadn't been as scary as he'd expected. The place was top-shelf, each lane topped with a comfortable seating area where black, cushiony leather seats surrounded a granite table. The waitresses were discrete, the drinks were stiff and the walls between each lane provided a private ambience that could almost put a man in mind of other entertainments if he were so inclined.

He and Edie were just starting the third game when she suggested a cash wager. At first, Tyler had declined, but then she stared him down until he decided it was rude not to accept. Hey, if she wanted to part ways with some cash, he was okay with that.

The next frame, she threw a gutterball, then a lucky spare, but Tyler followed it with a wicked split that he knocked out proudly.

Who knew that bowling could be this much fun?

And if Edie were making the game a little closer, well, victory would be that much sweeter. "You know, if you worked on your delivery, you might do better," he suggested, trying to be helpful.

As soon as he finished speaking, she turned and looked at him with amazingly vacant brown eyes. Too vacant, warned a voice in his head. This time, she pulled her right arm back, then followed through with a rocket shot that hung to the right, until the very last second when it hooked center...*dead center.*

Tyler watched as ten pins fell, hard and loud. The machine cleaned away the toppled pins, as well as the last bits of his toppled ego.

"Lucky shot," he called out, slightly juvenile, but the male ego was a fragile thing.

"Lucky?" she taunted, and then threw three consecutive strikes. Tyler kept his tongue glued firmly to the top of his mouth, resisting name-calling, insults, or anything that might indicate he wasn't able to lose with dignity.

He was down twenty-five pins when she missed her spare, and when she had her back to him, he did allow himself a smug smile. By the tenth and final frame, she had him beaten, and Tyler gallantly offered to double down.

Edie focused on him. "Sucker's bet," she said with a shrug. "You sure?"

"I'm sure," he said, and then took off his jacket and rolled up his sleeves. He was a world-class cardiac surgeon, had backed the Oilers long after the Earl Campbell years and damn it, there was no way he was getting beaten by a girl.

He bowled two strikes and a spare and was ahead by a dozen pins when she approached the line, wiggled her hips, started to pull her arm back, then stopped.

Patiently, Tyler waited. He could see she was getting nervous. Finally, she threw the ball and ended with a strike. Not bothering to hide her smile, she skipped to the high-backed leather couch, sat down next to him and crossed one long leg dramatically over the other. At this angle, he could see right up to the very tops of her thighs. She assumed he would ogle. However, Tyler was a gentleman, and he did not ogle. Much.

Completely aware of his weakness, she slapped a hand on his thigh. "You're up, sport."

Before he rose, her hand slipped higher, only a touch, but it was enough. Brain function ceased, and all remaining blood rushed to his cock.

"Cheap tricks," he whispered, and then promptly knocked down the one and two pins, leaving the rest standing, much like his cock. Her laughter should have egged him on, should have fired his competitive spirit. It should not have tightened his groin into something even more painful.

But it did.

"You're going down," she told him cheerfully, and he smiled, not so cheerfully.

"Maybe, but you'll love every minute," answered some other voice that wasn't Tyler's.

She pushed at her hair, once, twice, before the confidence returned. She missed an easy spare, and he shrugged apologetically when she sat down.

"Cheater," she muttered under her breath, and he patted her bare thigh.

She shot him a skeptical look under her lashes, and when she threw again, two more strikes followed.

Now the score was tied, and it was the ninth frame.

"You think you can win, buster?" she jeered, and he watched, completely unmoved as her confident little ass shifted against the black leather cushion.

"Why not?" he asked innocently.

"Ha! I'm two well-handled balls away from victory."

His scrotum tightened, which had been her intent, but he noticed that she shifted again. Oh, she didn't want him to see, but he knew.

"Your turn," she reminded him, and reluctantly he approached the line. Twice he checked over his shoulder, and she grinned and waved every time as if nothing was wrong.

He ended with a miserable spare. She was waiting when he returned to the table.

"I don't need underhanded maneuvers to win," she mocked, and he met her eyes coolly.

"Am I supposed to understand that?"

She leaned closer, and he smelled the sharp tang of her perfume, and before he could stop himself, he breathed deeply.

"Are you trying to be sneaky?" she asked, moving closer, her mouth, now only inches from his.

"No," he told her, since he was never sneaky.

"You don't need to lie." She kissed his mouth once, twice, before her lips grazed the base of his ear. "I like you bad. I like you sneaky. I like you dirty. It makes me wet, damp, drenched with the very idea of it."

As a medical professional, Tyler was aware of the various biological responses to arousal, so it was completely understandable when he took her mouth and pulled her firmly in his lap, that he did find that she was wet, drenched and not ice cold, but burning with heat. So much heat...

Feeling emboldened, he pushed a finger inside her, once, twice, more than satisfied with her tortured moan.

Her hips ground against his hard-on, not helping matters, and then she opened her eyes, sharp with desire. "I've got your ass now," she whispered with authority, taking a playful nip at his lower lip.

There were few men able to maneuver their hands in tight places and perform delicate procedures, but Tyler could.

"You think?" he asked, then slipped three ice cubes beyond the innocent blue polka-dots, burying them deep inside her.

Her eyes opened wide with shock, and she jumped up from his lap, bumping her leg on the table, before pulling her skirt low.

Feeling a profound sense of satisfaction, Tyler folded his arms across his chest, and watched as she walked stiffly to the line. Her previously, perky and confident ass noticeably shifting first with discomfort, then pleasure.

Oh, she must be miserable, he thought to himself. The human body was a miraculous thing, full of mystery and vulnerabilities. Nothing that a trained medical professional didn't know how to exploit.

He was so completely engrossed in the fantasy of her bowling shoes riding on his shoulders that he missed her first strike.

Another followed. Game over.

Edie returned to him, and yes, she was still moving uncomfortably, but before she sat, she discreetly adjusted her skirt. A less astute man might not have spotted her right hand disappearing for a moment, but then it reappeared, and apparently everything was restored to its proper place.

Damn it.

She curled her legs beneath her, and twinkled up at him. "Sorry about the loss. I hope you're not too...deflated."

Deflated? He was going to be stuck like this for another year. And it would be all her fault. Gallantly, Tyler took her hand, covered it with his own and then brought it to his lips.

Slowly, she smiled at him.

"So why don't you ask me back to your hotel?" she purred.

"I don't know if I can make it that far," he answered quite sincerely.

"We'll have to improvise," she told him, jerking her thumb in the direction of the nearest exit.

THEY'D TRAVELED SEVEN BLOCKS, yet still hadn't found un-adulterated privacy. Edie's gaze searched north toward the beaconing lights of the Empire State Building, south toward the financial district, west toward the skyscrapers of Jersey and then east toward major construction scaffolding.

Construction scaffolding had never seemed so romantic. She looked at Tyler, expecting him to bolt, to be too upstanding to make love amongst building supplies. However, he was two steps ahead of her...literally.

Grabbing her hand, he hurried around the corner and into the darkened alcove of a boarded-up bank. Tyler ducked behind the curtain of plastic sheeting and grasped Edie's shoulders.

"We're seventy blocks from my hotel room. I have no idea where your apartment is. I don't know New York, but right now, I'm a man on the edge. Please tell me that all of tonight's temptation was not just to hear me babble incoherently like I am now."

He seemed so adorable when mussed, so approachable, so human. The tie was loose, the eyes were wild but she knew with absolute certainty that if Edie Higgins wasn't ready for this, then Tyler would let her go without a word of complaint.

Not that she was that cruel.

Not that she was that pure.

Right now, all she wanted to feel was *him* inside her, not stupid ice. *Ice?* The memory of it still made her thighs scream.

Edie lunged for him, her fingers attacking the buttons on his shirt, pulling it loose from his perfectly pressed trousers. He slid her green T-shirt off one shoulder, pushing up her bra, before his mouth settled hungrily on her breast.

The hard pressure was exquisite, and she braced herself against the shell of an ATM machine, forgetting everything but the insistence of his mouth. Soft hair brushed against her breast, and she could smell the crisp scent of his cologne teasing her nose. Her body fell into the easy rhythm

Send For
2 FREE BOOKS
Today!

I accept your offer!

Please send me two
free Harlequin® Blaze®
novels and two mystery
gifts (gifts worth about $10).
I understand that these books
are completely free—even
the shipping and handling will
be paid—and I am under no
obligation to purchase anything, ever,
as explained on the back of this card.

About how many NEW paperback fiction books have you purchased in the past 3 months?

❏ 0-2   ❏ 3-6   ❏ 7 or more
FDCV   **FDC7**   **FDDK**

151/351 HDL

Please Print

FIRST NAME

LAST NAME

ADDRESS

APT.#   CITY

Visit us online at
www.ReaderService.com

STATE/PROV.   ZIP/POSTAL CODE

Offer limited to one per household and not applicable to series that subscriber is currently receiving.

Your Privacy—The Reader Service is committed to protecting your privacy. Our Privacy Policy is available online at www.ReaderService.com or upon request from the Reader Service. We make a portion of our mailing list available to reputable third parties that offer products we believe may interest you. If you prefer that we not exchange your name with third parties, or if you wish to clarify or modify your communication preferences, please visit us at www.ReaderService.com/consumerschoice or write to us at Reader Service Preference Service, P.O. Box 9062, Buffalo, NY 14269. Include your complete name and address.

© 2010 HARLEQUIN ENTERPRISES LIMITED. ® and ™ are trademarks owned and used by the trademark owner and/or its licensee. Printed in the U.S.A. ▲ Detach card and mail today. No stamp needed. ▲ H-B-05/11

The Reader Service—Here's how it works: Accepting your 2 free books and 2 free gifts (gifts valued at approximately $10.00) places you under no obligation to buy anything. You may keep the books and gifts and return the shipping statement marked "cancel". If you do not cancel, about a month later we'll send you 6 additional books and bill you just $4.24 each in the U.S. or $4.71 each in Canada. That is a savings of 15% off the cover price. It's quite a bargain! Shipping and handling is just 50¢ per book in the U.S. and 75¢ per book in Canada.* You may cancel at any time, but if you choose to continue, every month we'll send you 6 more books, which you may either purchase at the discount price or return to us and cancel your subscription.

*Terms and prices subject to change without notice. Prices do not include applicable taxes. Sales tax applicable in N.Y. Canadian residents will be charged applicable taxes. Offer not valid in Quebec. Credit or debit balances in a customer's account(s) may be offset by any other outstanding balance owed by or to the customer. Please allow 4 to 6 weeks for delivery. Offer available while quantities last. All orders subject to credit approval. Books received may not be as shown.

▼ If offer card is missing write to: The Reader Service, P.O. Box 1867, Buffalo, NY 14240-1867 or visit www.ReaderService.com ▼

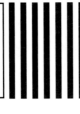

NO POSTAGE
NECESSARY
IF MAILED
IN THE
UNITED STATES

BUSINESS REPLY MAIL
FIRST-CLASS MAIL   PERMIT NO. 717   BUFFALO, NY

POSTAGE WILL BE PAID BY ADDRESSEE

THE READER SERVICE
PO BOX 1867
BUFFALO NY 14240-9952

of his mouth, her eyes drifting closed, floating away to someplace warm and exotic.

Edie groaned with delight, her body straining against him, greedy for his attention. The exquisite pressure grew more intense, more demanding, and she knew she would have done anything he wanted, given him anything he asked, if only he would finish this.

Finish her.

A moment later, his mouth left her breast. She regrettably restored her bra to rights, and then he leaned against her, his body imprinting itself on her. She could feel every strained tendon, the iron bands of his arms. Pressing insistently between her thighs was the flagrant manifestation of a man on the edge.

Oh, yes, solid and firm, here within her hands.

He kissed her with mouth and tongue, as if his life were ending soon, and she didn't understand why they weren't having sex yet.

"Not yet," he whispered against her mouth.

"When?"

"Truck."

His kisses were open-mouthed, hip-rolling instruments of torture, and she'd never liked torture. "Where?" she gasped, straddling his thigh in a shameless move for that very thing that she wanted. So badly. Right now.

Finally she heard the rolling thunder of the truck moving past.

"Now," she urged, as her hands delved below the belt, unloosening his pants, freeing the very heavy, very filling, very naughty part of him. In the darkness, her senses came alive as she felt the silky smooth flesh, the broad tip of his erection and the slight drop of liquid on the head. When he spoke, she could hear the strain in his voice, and she was pleased.

"I have a lot of concerns about this."

"You worried about getting caught?" she asked, her fingers stroking his cock, exploring the length, the breadth, the density and oh, la, la, the sensitivity.

"No," he answered, his voice low, pained.

"Then what?" she asked, teasing him with a lick of her tongue, and hearing the audible gasp. *Sweet*.

"You set me up."

Strain was no longer in his voice. Control was back. The scales of virtue were now tilting firmly in his favor. She slid the tip of her index finger around him once, part seduction, part punishment, and then stared up at him. "No, I didn't."

Gently he pushed away. "What happened to your earlier lessons in courtship? What happened to knowing her personality, her heart? Why does *this* feel like another assembly-line product designed to express your deepest emotional connection?"

"Don't throw my words back at me."

"Why not? You seemed really fond of them earlier." He reordered his pants, his shirt, his tie, his white-knight outlook on life.

A chill set in, not a summer breeze, but the aching knowledge that Tyler Hart wasn't going to play by her rules. At least not yet. "What do you want, Tyler?" she asked, her voice unsteady...*and weak*. "What the hell is wrong with sex?"

"On a street corner? Against an ATM?"

"This was your idea," she reminded him.

"It was a bad one."

"It was a great one."

"Why can't we do this right?" he said with a sigh, and then pushed her hair back from her face, because even when he was ruining her plans, he still had to be the gentleman.

"There is no right. There is no wrong. Sex is sex."

This time he shoved a hand through his own hair and began to pace. "I'm not talking about sex, Edie. You said you would teach me all the crappy emotional stuff. Don't get me wrong, I love the sex. I adore the sex. I want the sex, but my last girlfriend cheated on me, and all you want to do is jump me, and now I'm worried that you were right and I'm a brick. I'm tired of being an emotional brick. Bricks are not good."

Her mouth opened, then closed. "You're not a brick."

"I think you're saying that only because you don't want to teach me the crappy emotional stuff."

"You can't keep calling it the crappy emotional stuff."

"See? I'm a brick."

Edie felt something melt inside her, since he was a brick, but he was a very appealing brick. She understood that frustration—the feeling that something was off inside, but having no idea how to fix it. Edie pretended it didn't exist, but not so Tyler. No, Tyler had to do the hard time and be the better person. Taking very small steps, Edie went to him and wrapped her arms around him. As a rule, she was a hugger because people responded well to touching. However, this was different. This was hard.

Slowly, his arms crept around her.

"I have nothing against kissing," she muttered.

"Kissing leads to sex."

"I've heard that's not always true."

"Okay," he murmured, paying appropriate homage to her neck. So Edie stood quietly, straining to hear the wind slapping the plastic sheeting, straining to hear the last of the late-night traffic, but instead hearing nothing apart from the sure beating of his heart. This was kissing. This was courtship. This was the very emotional crap that she feared.

Many minutes passed, forever maybe, and she stayed there until he took her arm and led her east. Silently they walked farther north to where the lights of New Jersey reflected on the water. A long greenway separated the street from the Hudson, a line of hedges and trees and benches all designed to mask the docks, mask the garbage plant and mask the long barges that glided slowly in the night.

"Here," announced Tyler, sitting down on a bench and looking at her expectantly.

"What?"

"I think you're supposed to sit next to me and then we're supposed to watch the changing landscape."

Edie threw out a dramatic hand, encompassing most of the tristate area. "This is not landscape. This is industrial camouflage, nothing more. You're just fooled because you're a starry-eyed tourist."

Tyler started to laugh. Stubbornly she still refused to sit, tapping her foot against the industrial pavement. "Well, you are," she insisted. Tyler stared up at her with that knowing look, that frankly wasn't starry-eyed at all. Eventually nervously, she sat...a good two feet away from him.

"All right. Go ahead. What did you want to discuss?"

"Why don't you sleep?"

"I don't know what you're talking about," she told him, glancing at her watch, wishing the dawn could come up a little faster.

"You do these all-nighters often?"

"No," she lied.

"It's almost five a.m., you haven't had any caffeine, your pupils aren't dilated and I haven't seen you yawn once. Ergo, your body's clock isn't running anywhere close to normal."

"You're in the city that never sleeps. They don't call it that for nothing."

"Don't you ever get tired?" he asked, and she realized that yes, she was exhausted.

She inched closer to him, and some of her industrial

camouflage fell away. "I get tired sometimes," she said, and he pulled her close to him, wrapping an arm around her, and pushing her head into his shoulder. It was a comfortable shoulder, strong, too possibly available for crying if one were into crying—which Edie was not. But it was nice to know he had good shoulders.

"I suppose as a curator, you're not used to long hours or a hectic lifestyle," she whispered.

"You should take pity on me."

Pity? No, never that. "You're lucky I don't think you're boring," she teased.

"I am boring."

"You? Are you kidding?" She adjusted just so that she could goggle at him. "Not even close."

He smiled at her, and she noticed the crinkly lines around his eyes. He had good eyes, too—if a woman was into that, which Edie wasn't.

"I like this industrial camouflage. It's so quiet here."

She blew an inelegant raspberry. "Well, yeah, if you ignore the early morning delivery trucks, the fire engines and the bicyclists."

He shot her a sideways look. "Bicyclists don't make noise."

"They do when they have bells," she said, and as if to prove her point, a sleekly clad cyclist zoomed by, brrr-ring the tinny chime, as if Edie or Tyler were going to suddenly throw themselves into oncoming bicycle traffic. Puh-lease. Bikers could be so full of themselves.

"You're not big on bikes, are you?"

"No." There, she'd lied again because it was only a twisted person who didn't like bicycles. They were great exercise, energy efficient, a multi-age mode of transportation that was both cheap and easy, and they came in all sorts of pretty colors. Not liking bikes was right up there with not liking Monopoly, not liking chocolate ice cream, or not liking Santa Claus.

"Didn't you ever want one?" he asked.

Hell, yeah. Edie had desperately wanted a bicycle when she was seven because to her childish, naive eyes, a bicycle seemed like the answer to all her prayers. Considering how she had begged and hinted for days at a time, it was no surprise that her father had been suckered in and bought one. Bright and early on Christmas morning, Edie had raced down the stairs, there it was under the Christmas tree.

A bike. Her bike. Flashy chrome trim, twelve speeds, disc brakes, all mounted on a diamond-bright, sparkling blue frame that dazzled the eyes. It was the most beautiful thing she'd ever seen.

However, there was a downside to the bike-plan. Edie couldn't ride a bike. She didn't have a clue. The only reason she'd wanted the stupid thing in the first place was to force her father to teach her how to ride me. To force him to spend some quality time with her. And did Dr. Jordan Higgins, M.D., Ph.D., IQ off the charts clue in? Oh, no.

Her mother had trudged in that afternoon and dutifully volunteered to teach Edie to ride. But Edie had burst into tears, her mother had stroked her hair and the bicycle disappeared the next day.

Bikes were crap.

"Why do I need a bike? A bicycle is a huge pain in the city. Why ride when you have the subway, or cabs, or your feet?" She dangled her flamingo sandals under the bench, and Tyler laughed.

"I figured that you'd want something a little faster. Something that wouldn't make you dependent on someone else."

"Well, you'd figure wrong."

"We should bike in Central Park," he announced, and she shot him a hell-no look.

"Why not?" he asked, a perfectly reasonable question.

"It's very pedestrian," she explained.

"Ha. What's the real problem? Bad fall?" he asked, sensing that she was fudging the truth. She liked that about him, that he understood her bullshit ways and didn't give up on her, but kept patiently pressing her until she came clean.

"There is no problem."

"Chicken?" he taunted.

"Not even close."

"So you'll go?"

"I didn't say that."

"So you're chicken?"

"No. I'm not."

"Edie. What's the hang-up here?"

The night had almost completely faded, she could feel the warmth of the early morning sun on her back. Everything seemed so much easier in the daytime. Everything seemed so possible. Or maybe that was due to Tyler.

She drew a deep breath, having decided to share. "For your information, there are certain talents that are not necessary to an average New Yorker. Most do not have a driver's license. Most do not cook. Most do not do their own laundry even. And most are never taught to ride a bicycle."

His mouth fell open in shock…mock shock. "You're joking? You can't ride a bike!"

She jabbed him in the ribs, mock hard. "Don't be mean. It doesn't become you."

"It's not mean. I'm just…surprised. I figured somebody like you would want to learn these things."

"Maybe," she hedged.

"You want to learn, don't you?" he asked, meeting her eyes. Quickly, she looked away.

"At twenty-eight? No, thank you."

"Okay."

Just Surrender...

"See. You didn't even want to teach me."

"I did. I do. We need a plan. A goal. A race."

"Next month is a big organized ride through the city. But would you really teach me?"

"Oh, yeah, sure. It'd be great, a nice change of pace. Not bowling. Not strip clubs. Bicycling. You should know that I'm very good at biking, but I'll let you ride ahead the whole way."

"That's so thoughtful of you."

"As long as you wear the tight black shorts," he added.

"This is all one big excuse to play Texas grab-ass, isn't it?" she lectured, which would have sounded more chaste if she hadn't been the one doing the ass grabbing earlier. Hopefully, he'd have forgotten that one minor point.

When he leaned in, there was acknowledgment in his eyes, that said, oops, he remembered. It was a testament to her newly found positive outlook that she didn't mind. "Why don't I come back with you to the hotel? I'll show you how much fun Texas grab-ass can be."

"Oh, yeah..." he began and then stopped. "I can't. Working tomorrow."

No, she wasn't disappointed. She didn't need to care, and her lustily throbbing loins would wait for another day. She rose to her feet, taking a deep breath of industrial camouflage. It wasn't so bad after all. If he wanted to learn the emotional crap, then she'd teach him. It'd take him all of ten minutes to learn. For Edie, it would take another ten years. But she chose not to mention that.

"Save all your cowboy bluster for Monday. You're going to need it for karaoke."

He didn't seem nearly so enthused. "Karaoke? You really don't mean that."

"I do. I have a book club meeting first, something for the ladies at work, but after that we'll see what you're made of." Then she pressed a kiss to his cheek, then flashed her dimples in her most engaging manner. "Don't tell me you're chicken," she chided, her sandaled-feet already taking her home.

"Not chicken. More…smart. You don't want to hear me sing," he called.

"Bricks can't sing, either. Don't be a brick," she called in return, feeling the first golden rays on her shoulders. As she walked off into the sunrise, she couldn't resist one last glance. Tyler Hart, even scared stiff, was the best fun a girl could ever have.

9

THE ST. AGNES HOSPITAL complex was like a mini-city on the Upper East Side. The four campuses were each world-renowned in their own right: the teaching hospital, the research laboratories, the cancer unit and the cardiac unit. When Tyler had been offered a full scholarship to med school at Baylor, he'd almost turned it down. Baylor? Certainly, it was good, but after spending his formative years in the sticks of West Texas, Tyler wanted the prestige of the big, nationally known hospitals: Johns Hopkins, Mayo, Duke or Mass General. While the other kids memorized baseball stats or starting offensive lines, Tyler had locked himself in his room with the *New England Journal of Medicine*. However, Baylor University was no Acme Medicine, and Tyler had done his time, finished first in his class and schemed, strategized and upgraded his social skills, all in preparation for Phase II: Dr. Tyler Hart, The Residency.

During his fourth year, he'd campaigned hard for a residency at New York Presbyterian, but on Match Day, when the letters were handed out, it was Max Lockwood who was going to Manhattan, and Tyler was bound for—*wait for it*—Houston.

The next twenty-four hours passed in a haze of alcohol and depression, as Tyler poured over his obviously lacking transcripts. In the end, he'd found himself at University of Texas at Houston, studying cardiology under the demanding leadership of Dr. Richard Stringer. On the first day, Dr. Stringer gave them all a cup of coffee and then explained to his bright-eyed interns that perfection wasn't nearly good enough. God had the luxury of letting his patients die. A doctor had to be better, smarter, steadier. A doctor had to work the miracles that God had denied. The interns glanced nervously at each other, pretending this was no big deal and the day went downhill from there.

The next few years were a sleepless blur, but in the process, Tyler discovered something fascinating. He loved surgery, he loved the power, the absoluteness, the correctness.

Now it was Sunday afternoon, and he was lucky enough to be in New York, making the rounds with the greatest surgeon ever to have grafted a vein, Dr. Abe Keating. After finishing up a consult on a seventy-three-year-old prime minister with endocarditis, Tyler walked with Dr. Keating, trying to keep the awe from his voice. When they rounded a corner, Keating froze in his tracks. Tyler stared in growing disbelief, watching as Dr. Keating greeted the approaching doctor.

"Max!" bellowed Dr. Keating. "How the hell are you?"

"Sorry I missed the opening kickoff. Damned airlines. Prescott Medical had flown me out to St. Barts. New product. NDA. The weather was a bitch and we just got in this morning." Lockwood—the weasel—then stared and sneered at Tyler. "Tyler. Fancy seeing you in Yankee country."

"Max," Tyler replied tensely.

Since apparently once wasn't good enough, Dr. Keating slapped Max on the back again, nodded absently in Tyler's general direction and said, "I'll let you guys catch up. Max, we'll talk more about Prescott. Maybe drinks at the club? You can give me some advice," Keating added, punctuating it with another pat on his back. "I think I need a wife. Sixty-two isn't too old, is it?"

"Not at all, sir," gushed Tyler sincerely, but Keating was already gone.

Max was grinning at Tyler as if he were happy. "Son of a bitch. How long has it been?" he asked.

"If it hasn't been two centuries, it hasn't been long enough."

Max burst out laughing. "You're here for the fellowship?"

"Not for drinks at the club. Some of us actually do practice medicine."

"I've missed your dedication," Max told him with the practiced sincerity of a surgeon.

"Yeah, it was the only way you passed organic."

"You were just jealous because the TA slept with me."

"I wanted to be a surgeon, not a prostitute," Tyler answered sanctimoniously because cheating could be forgiven, having a better personality could be forgiven, but stealing Tyler's slot at NY-Presby? Hell would freeze first.

"Touchy, aren't we? Hubris was always your problem. Too bad there's no Greek gods to smack you down for it. You honestly think you've got a shot at winning the endowment? After two months of Keating admiring my surgical techniques, it's my name that's going to be on the plaque down in the lobby. It's Dr. Max Lockwood who's going to beat you out of this prestigious post."

Tyler lifted a brow. "I read your last write-up in the journal. Sloppy."

Max's eyes narrowed. "Your patents mean nothing to me."

"And the consulting deal I signed with Pulmonary Horizons?"

For the first time, Tyler saw the cold fear in Max's face. "P.H.? Really? You've been busy."

Tyler glanced around the hallway and then smiled in a completely friendly manner. "I won't lose again, Max. I respect you, admire you, think you're a helluva surgeon, but this time, I'm going to kick your ass."

Max shook his head. "Don't get your heart set on the endowment, big guy. Although, hey, if you're going to get killed, I suppose a hospital is the place to be."

"You were always too smug, Lockwood."

"Not without cause," Max boasted, but a hint of anxiety had crept into his eyes. "Did you scrub in on the Fogelman surgery?"

"Of course. I didn't see you there."

"I got there before the crowds," answered Max, checking his pager as if he were in demand.

"Bastard," muttered Tyler, checking his pager, as well.

"Keating's opening up the prime minister tomorrow at nine a.m."

"It's at eight," Tyler corrected smoothly. "And I didn't see your name on the list."

Max shrugged as only the guilty can. "It was worth a shot."

"You're not going to catch me snoozing this time."

"I earned that fellowship fair and square."

"It was my technique," Tyler reminded him.

"We worked on it together," argued Max, who never shared the limelight well.

"Slacker," returned Tyler.

"Bastard."

Realizing that if he was intent on giving Max the smackdown he so desperately deserved, Tyler was going to have to work a little harder. Not a problem. "It's good to see you again, Limpwood. Prepare to be vanquished."

Max shot him the finger, but Tyler strolled off in too good of a mood. Great sex with Edie, a little competition to keep him on his toes and cracking open the human chest cavity in order to fix what God had ignored.

No, life didn't get better than this.

LADY JANE'S SALON WAS a throwback to a long-lost era when women giggled while fluttering fans, and if a man ruined a lady's reputation, the town branded him a rapscallion, not a hero on Facebook. Low-slung velvet sofas were scattered around the room to encourage conversation. Gilt portraits of ladies of questionable virtue hung from the flocked-wallpaper walls. It was the type of place where woman ordered Singapore Slings and the bartenders wore tuxes. In short, it was the last bastion of romance in a city of cynics. Yes, it was also the least likely place for a women's solidarity book club, but it was Edie's favorite spot, and since this was her book club, she got to make the rules. Earlier that afternoon, she had prepared what she hoped was a stimulating treatise on *Jane Eyre*.

Tonight's group was Edie, Wanda, Olga and Honey. According to Wanda, Patience had a date with someone new, a man she'd met at the bowling alley, not that Edie was the least bit surprised. After a few minutes of casual conversation, the drinks were ordered and Edie called for everyone's attention. She was halfway through the comparison of Jane's journey to a modern woman's misguided and often tragic search for true love, when Olga interrupted, choosing to shoot holes in Edie's theory. "Edie, why don't you give Jane a break?"

Edie laughed knowingly. Olga's knee-jerk reaction was typical of women who chose to overindulge the male figures in their life. "How many think Jane is heroic?" she said, asking for a quick show of hands.

Three glasses raised high and Edie nodded. "Now, how many of you think Jane was a victim, whose only purpose in life was to be rescued by men over and over, rather than a role model of trail-blazing courage whose pathway was one of her own choosing?"

There were some rumblings of discontent about that provocative line of reasoning, and one eavesdropping gentleman even disagreed, as well. But Edie had expected this sort of blowback, so she continued to illustrate her point. "Let's discuss the childhood years. Our intrepid heroine is abused, bullied and locked in her room until she faints. Dude says, 'Go to school.' She's all 'Oh, gee, what a great idea,' and then leaves. Proactive? Taking charge? My ass is more proactive than that. And the years Jane spends at Lowood? It's like *Oliver Twist,* only instead of 'More, please' it's 'Jane, you ignorant slut.' Who rescues her this time? Miss Temple, that's who, and to top it all off, Helen dies. Is that courage because she chooses to suffer with silent dignity? Antiquated, that's what that is."

"I thought it was classy," defended Wanda—Wanda, of all people, who complained about her husband Harry on a daily basis.

Edie rolled her eyes. "And you would be the first one going after Mr. Brocklehurst with a cane."

Wanda shook her head, still not convinced. "Doesn't mean that she wasn't classy."

Realizing that this was going to be more difficult than she anticipated, Edie rushed onward to point number three. "Thornfield Hall? She's a governess who falls for her married employer, who is keeping his crazy wife locked in the attic. And she thinks he's a prize."

"He couldn't help his wife's condition," argued Honey,

taking a demure sip from her mojito, all while keeping a watchful eye on the flirty dude in the corner.

Edie leaned forward, if only to break up the eye-sex. "He could have told Jane what was going on. 'Oh, that crazy laughter. You know, that's my wife.' But did he think about coming clean? Hell, no."

"He was in love with her," Honey said. "He knew the truth would keep them apart."

"No, his jerkiness would keep them apart," Edie insisted valiantly, apparently the only one in the room who considered honesty a requirement before falling in love.

"She did save Rochester from a fire," Olga added.

"You know what would have been better? If she had loved him, lost him in the fire, and after learning from the experience then reclaimed the life she should have had all along."

"That's very cynical," argued Honey, who was a twenty-three-year-old stripper who made a six-figure income—mostly in cash.

Edie sighed, and motioned the bartender for another round. "Honey, describe your ideal man."

"That's easy," she answered. "Good sense of humor. Smart. Responsible. A good dresser. I like men in suits."

Wanda and Olga nodded in agreement.

"But you didn't say a word about how he would treat you."

Honey smiled patiently, as if Edie was the one who was slow. "That's implied. He'd send me flowers and take me to shows and shower me with oodles of compliments."

Edie whacked herself on the forehead. "No, no, no. These are shallow gestures that the patriarchy has defined for us in lieu of an equitable partnership. Flowers? Give me a break. What if he showed up early instead of late? What if he walked the dog? Or changed a tire?"

"Harry doesn't change tires," complained Wanda. "He's

says, 'I got Triple A for that.' And we don't even have a car."

"I think Mr. Rochester would change a tire," Honey rationalized, still defending the world's sorriest excuse for a hero.

"Tires did not exist in 1847," Olga explained.

"They had wheels," Honey argued. "Mr. Rochester would change a wheel for Jane."

"And maybe he would," Edie agreed, "but he still wanted Jane to run away with him."

Even Wanda took the opposing side. "So they could be together. There's nothing wrong with that, Edie."

"He could have offed his wife," Olga suggested. "Then they would be free to be together."

"Ladies, I think we're missing the big picture. Mr. Rochester is not a good person."

Wanda cast a disapproving eye at Edie. "He loved Jane."

"He lied to Jane."

"He thought she would be freaked out by his injured repulsiveness."

"Because yes, once again, Jane is thrust into the role of a caretaker, until, gee willikers, his sight magically appears."

If Tyler were here, he would be on Edie's side. Tyler was a very sensible man. Frankly, the world needed more sensible men.

"Jane could have studied to be an eye surgeon. They can do wonders these days. I saw this piece on *Sixty Minutes*..." Honey trailed off when the bartender appeared with their drinks, and it was then that Edie abandoned all hope of education.

They were hopeless. All of them. Including Edie, most of all. She had counted on the group to support her position because in a mere two hours and thirty-seven minutes, she would be meeting a man who made her heart beat a little faster, a little happier. Normally this would not worry her. She often had great times with men. But not men like Tyler. He worried her, these expectations worried her. He thought she was capable of teaching him great things. As for Edie, her expectations for Tyler were rocketing toward the stratosphere, and frankly, she wasn't a stratosphere kind of gal.

Noticing Edie's sad face, Wanda came over and sat next to her. "You know we're just giving you a hard time because it's fun."

"I don't think we're ever going to learn, Wanda. I think we're destined to get heartbroken over and over again, because the X chromosome has doormat written all over it."

"Olga said he changed your tire," Wanda said, as if that made being a doormat somehow acceptable.

"It was Barnaby's tire."

Olga shot Edie a sympathetic smile. "Does he have a mad wife?"

"No, only an ex-girlfriend by the name of Cynthia," explained Edie, because she needed to remain rational, grounded, and not worry about whether her red halter dress was appropriate for karaoke later.

"At least he didn't lie to you," Honey offered, defending the man who needed no defending at all.

Out of all of her friends, Wanda was the oldest, the wisest, and the one who could see through Edie the best. "Why don't you want to like him?" she asked.

Edie considered her answer very carefully. There was a time when Edie would have lied to preserve her image, when she would have brushed it off with a wink and a laugh, but things inside her were starting to change. She told herself it was age, she told herself it was experience.

Neither of which were true, and she knew it, but she wasn't
ready to think about that. Not yet.

"I do like him. He's completely not my type, but he's
very likeable. Have you ever met someone like that? That
you don't want to like, but damn them, they make you?"

"Harry," muttered Wanda.

"Paco," murmured Olga.

"Edward," crooned Edie.

All around them, the room was full of people searching
for that intangible something, that mysterious someone, and
they were willing to take a leap of faith that the stranger
in front of them was someone who was worthy of the risk.
Edie had spent her entire young-adult years disapproving
of her mother's silent suffering, and even that didn't stop
the first, ill-fated flutterings for Tyler. She had dreamed
of love, she had idealized love, but when push came to
shove, she didn't want to be the woman left sitting alone
at night.

Wanda patted her hand. "Don't beat yourself up, Edie.
The heart knows what it knows."

"The heart is a senseless organ."

"But necessary."

"We have a date," Edie confessed, her senseless organ
joyously leaping at the words.

Honey—who wasn't seasoned enough to sense what an
absolute betrayal this was to Edie's entire belief system—
sparkled with excitement for her. "When?"

Edie checked her watch, mentally reminding herself
that this was no big deal. Casual. Carefree. *Liar.* "In an
hour."

Honey glanced over the halter dress with a critical eye.
"You're going in that?"

At the innocent question, the doubts started, the worries
began and the dry heaves collected in Edie's stomach. "It's

my best nondate, date dress. Not too sincere, not too trashy. It says fun and carefree. It says 'I'm not Jane Eyre.'"

"It goes well with that gleam in your eye," Wanda told her, smiling.

"What gleam?" asked Edie, praying such a gleam wasn't serious recognition of something else.

Wanda shook her head and started to laugh. "Hope, darling. We call that hope."

MONDAY NIGHT KARAOKE had a dedicated following of fans who were much like Monday night football fans, much like European soccer fans, and eerily similar to those brave, yet mostly stupid souls who risked life and limb to follow twisters. When listening to the singers, Edie never booed, nor heckled. She enjoyed hearing the ear-splitting train wrecks, if only to appreciate her life a little bit more.

She arrived a half hour early, picked a circular table in the back, ordered a tonic water and wiped her sweaty palms on the cocktail napkin, resisting the urge to shred the paper into small pieces. There were a few familiar faces in the crowd, and she waved, not as friendly as normal, earning her some questioning looks because Edie was always friendly, always welcoming and never nervous.

Except when she was on a date.

Everything was so much easier when there were no expectations. Pre-Tyler, Edie was a master of low expectations. There was a certain comfort and consistency in believing the worst in people. You did not hurt and you were never disappointed—both big wins in Edie's book. Post-Tyler...

Post-Tyler? It had been four days. What should have been a non-life-changing four days. Pre-Tyler, Edie had scoffed at those women who were willing to rearrange their lives, their schedules and their hearts for a man. She especially scoffed at those women who would exhibit these behaviors after only a mere four days. Or redefine their life into phases, like Pre-Tyler, or Post-Tyler. Now she was one of them.

Quickly, she glanced around the room in case anyone was scoffing at her. Although they weren't, frankly, she thought they should because she wasn't comfortable with this vulnerability that sat upon her like a wet blanket.

It made her uncomfortable because now Edie wanted to believe. Wanted to believe that people didn't have to disappoint her. Wanted to believe in the basic unselfishness of the human heart.

Wanted to believe in pink unicorns, too, she thought with a mental eye-roll.

Emotional shenanigans, that's what this was. Emotional shenanigans that were making her stomach pitch and roll like Jane Eyre waiting for Mr. Rochester.

Instead of focusing on the rolling waves in her stomach, Edie told herself to focus on the couple at the table next to her. They were middle-aged and newly divorced...not from each other. The man wore a funeral-looking suit, and kept pulling nervously at his ear. The woman was wearing a hideously flowered-polyester dress in a very flattering shade of blue. Predictably, neither knew how to converse, and Edie listened to the painfully awkward conversation of two people who had no idea how to transcend the cheap meaningless relationships of a technologically savvy, yet emotionally marooned society.

When the woman left for the restroom, Edie saw her opening and tapped the gentleman on the back, smiling nicely. "Can I offer some advice?"

His eyes widened in fear, which said much about his state of anxiety since Edie was perhaps the least intimidating human being alive, and her words sounded like neither a sales pitch nor an intro to a religious conversion. Eventually, he realized that she was waiting politely for his answer, so he nodded once, his Adam's apple bobbing rapidly.

"She's as nervous as you are," Edie told him in a confidential tone. "Here's what you do. Tell her that you're terrified that you'll screw this up, and she seems very nice, and you don't want to screw it up. Make up a code word— *'gobsmacked'* is good—and tell her that if you start saying anything goofy, embarrassing, or strange, she needs to say 'gobsmacked,' so that you'll know to stop. And ask about her job. Don't talk about yours unless she asks. Remember, she's priority one. Tomorrow, you can go back to me-me-me, but for these next few hours, it's all about her."

"Why are you telling me this?" the gentleman asked suspiciously, because only in New York did people question whether the milk of human kindness had been spiked with poison.

"Why? Because you picked karaoke, which is strike one for a first date. You're wearing a funeral suit, which is strike two, and I think she likes you, which means almost all strikes can be forgiven."

"Really?"

"Yes. She's here with you, isn't she? That says something." Then Edie gave him a gentle, reassuring smile. Such an innocent lamb. It was touching, in an "I hope no one serves you for dinner" sort of way.

The man blinked twice and adjusted his tie, as if he still wasn't convinced, but when his date returned, he leaned closer and began talking. Sure enough, the woman laughed, and Edie blew the end of an imaginary revolver, gunslinger-style. She, the righter of wrongs and the corrector of possibly aberrant human behaviors. Frankly, the world didn't know how totally screwed it up it was. Another singer took to the tiny stage and secretly Edie checked the time, not that she expected Tyler to be early, but yes, she expected that Tyler would be early. Then she laughed at her own goofiness.

At five to eight, she could feel her heartbeat accelerating with anticipation, and she watched the trio of frat boys serenading a very pretty, very embarrassed girl in the corner. It was sweet and funny, and almost enough to get her mind off the clock. Almost. At eight-fifteen, a distinguished elderly gentleman came to her table and asked if she needed company.

"I'm waiting for someone," she told him firmly, and watched as he shuffled off to talk to the next single woman in the room. All around her, people were trying to make connections. Before she had secretly scoffed. Now she was part of the whole messy business.

At eight-thirty, she began to worry that Tyler was trapped in a cab, stuck somewhere on the thruway and heading north to Albany. Not being from New York, he wouldn't know that he was moving in the wrong direction. Edie told herself to get a grip.

At eight-forty-five, she reset her phone, just in case she had missed a call, or a text message, or a traffic update indicating all bridges and tunnels were closed because the UN was in session, the president had decided to drop by Broadway, or Jack Bauer was helicoptering in to save the world.

None seemed likely.

All around her people were trying to make connections, but it was Edie, the righter of wrongs, the corrector of possibly aberrant human behaviors, who had failed.

Her smile drifted in the downward direction and she smiled at the music while quietly shredding her napkin to bits.

At nine o'clock, she was already in the fourth stage of grief—depression—having moved past denial, anger and bargaining. It spoke volumes about Tyler's character that

Edie had taken an entire hour to advance this far in the process. Usually she zoomed straight past anger to acceptance, because depression over someone else's faults was a depressing waste of time. Life was too short to get hung up on the disappointments, but she still couldn't leave.

When her watch said nine-thirty, she rose from her seat, as if she were going to high-tail it out this joint and find a real party. Pre-Tyler, that's exactly what she would have done. But now it felt as if she had a care in the world, and frankly, it sucked.

Slowly, she sat down, and then tapped her fingers in time to the music, which, considering the vocal skills of the singers, was not as easy as Edie had hoped, but she managed. Anything to avoid dwelling on Tyler's betrayal.

Except that he had seemed so thoughtful, so considerate, so polite. Tyler Hart was the man least likely to stand up a woman. She'd seen the pained anxiety when he'd talked to his ex. And what if he was back with his ex? Edie brooded, now openly dwelling on Tyler's betrayal.

No. He would have said something. Tyler was nothing if not excruciatingly, self-sacrificingly honest. Tyler would have twisted himself into knots in order to do the right thing. Which meant that somehow, in between the sex and the bowling and the flat tire and the sex and the bench-talking and the sex, she had begun to give him the benefit of the doubt.

Did great sex justify such a generous benefit of the doubt? No, she decided flatly. Benefit of the doubt only led to foolishly overlooking very real character flaws, which led to an endless barrage of excuses for someone who didn't deserved them, which eventually led to an endless barrage of excuses for yourself. No, great sex wasn't worth that. Nothing was worth that.

"Is this seat taken?"

The voice belonged to a twentysomething kid, who on

an ordinary night, she would have invited to sit and chat, coax him into a long discussion on the girls that he loved, or listen to his dreams and smile politely, but Edie didn't want to listen to someone else's dreams.

"I'm waiting for my father," she told him. "We're lovers," she added with a whisper, watching his look of horror with what some might term unholy glee. Usually she shocked people for attention, but not now. She didn't have the energy to morph herself into some image of what the kid wanted her to be, and wound licking was best done alone. The kid left to find some other attractive twentysomething who wasn't quite so particular. Good luck with that.

The hours ticked by, and she told herself that she was enjoying the music, enjoying the solitude, but after listening to seven different versions of "Living On a Prayer," she was still checking her watch, she was still glancing anxiously toward the door. What she needed was one last nail in her coffin. Some kind of a sharp reminder. Edie picked up her phone and dialed.

"Dad?"

"Edie? Is that you?"

"Happy anniversary, Dad," she told him, which could be interpreted in many ways. A thoughtful wishing of good fortune to someone she genuinely loved. A subliminal dagger designed to remind said paternal unit of his failings in his familial responsibilities. Or a polite conversation opener when no more sincere words could be found. The actual truth was that it was some sort of dysfunctional mash-up of all three.

"You sound sincere," her father said easily. "Thank you."

Not wanting him to overlook the first two meanings, Edie said, "You don't have to thank me because your anniversary was Friday and you stood Mom up, and paid Mary Helen to send her a card."

Her father laughed because theirs was a complicated relationship best left undisturbed by momentary flashes of mawkish sentimentality that might confuse the more conflicted reality. "Now that's the Edie I know and love. Where would I be without you to keep me humble?"

Where would he be without her? In exactly the same place that he was. Edie had not altered his life in any manner, no matter how foolishly she tried. At last, peace flowed through her. Acceptance.

On the stage, a woman began to croon her own special rendition of "My Heart Will Go On," and Edie pressed forward. "I called to see if you wanted to have lunch."

"Lunch? I'd love to. What day are you free?"

"Any day, really." The great thing about owning a diner that employed twice the staff that it should was that it gave Edie oodles and oodles of free time in which to rescue the world.

"Let me check the calendar," her father said, and then paused. "Holy mackerel, where did Mary Helen put my calendar? Aha! Found it. So, Edie wants to have lunch. Can't do Wednesday, there's a meeting with the business development department, and those are never fun. Never short, either. And tomorrow I'll be in surgery. Although if I get lucky and get out early, I could give you a call. Saturday is out. Dr. Keating is coming in to brief me on the new fellowship candidates. On Thursday there's a golf game at Scarsdale. Don't want to miss that one. Norm's putting down hard cash on the game, and he gave me a five-stroke handicap. Like I need a handicap. Let's see... Friday? Another surgery. This one will be a doozy. They're filming it for the Discovery Channel. Can you believe that, Edie? Your old man's going to be on TV."

Edie listened to the wispy strains of the melody and smiled to herself because there was nothing like a parent to put things in proper perspective. "You know, don't worry about lunch, Dad."

"But what about tomorrow?"

"Call me if you finish in time," she offered, gazing at the doorway, knowing that she'd been stood up, knowing her father wouldn't be there for lunch, and wishing that neither reality hurt so badly.

"I will. You know I'm good for it. Say, do you know what your mother would want for her anniversary? Sure, it's a little late, but better late than never."

"She already bought herself a present, Dad," she told him, and her father laughed.

"Whew. Dodged a bullet there. Guess she knows me too well. Oh, oops. There's the pager. Gotta go. Love you, Edie. And remember, we'll do lunch tomorrow."

"'Bye, Dad," she whispered, because he had already hung up.

"Can I buy you a drink?" asked skeevy man, apparently on the make for vulnerable females with shredded napkins.

"I'm great, thanks," she told him, sliding the incriminating napkin bits into her purse.

"You look sad," he said, claiming the spot next to her as if she needed the company.

"I'm great, thanks," she repeated, a little more forcefully, hoping he would pick up on the "I want to be alone" tone in her voice.

"Seriously. I know you could use somebody to talk to," he answered, missing the "I want to be alone" tone in her voice, possibly because Edie never used an "I want to be alone" tone and ergo had no idea what it was supposed to sound like.

"I don't think so," she insisted, because Edie never needed anyone to talk to. Edie was the counselor, the listener, the fixer. Edie was never the one with the problem. Ever.

"Seriously," he repeated, so completely sure that she needed someone tonight.

She shot him a hard smile. "*Seriously.* I'm giving you a chance to back out gracefully. I'm a cop. Undercover. This is an undercover prostitution sting. Feel like getting busted?"

Instantly, he backed away, and Edie wished that just once the world would surprise her. But no. Melty-eyed men with an earnest voice were apparently no different than any other male of the species. They were only attuned to their own primordially dictated instincts.

To thine own self be true; screw everybody else.

Right then, a shadow fell across the table. Her goddamned heart leaped—*leaped*—as if it might still be Tyler. Covering quickly she beamed up at Patience and Wanda, who sat down on either side to her. When the waiter approached, they ordered a round of drinks that involved both large amounts of sugar and alcohol, and had sexy names, like Run, Skip and Go Naked and Screaming Orgasm, as if one hundred proof could be a surrogate for a romantic companionship. Very astute, those drink-naming marketing types. After the drinks arrived, Edie absently twirled the fragile pink paper umbrella, watching it collapse under pressure. Across the table, Patience fiddled with her napkin, shredding it into small pieces.

"I thought you had a date," she told Patience.

"*Date?* Did you know that date was a four-letter word? He wanted to go bowling again. Why did I think it would be fun to date a man whose idea of a fantastic night out is a trip to the bowling alley?"

Tyler didn't bowl for fun, but he did know how to have a good time at it. Edie pushed the thought aside. "If I were you, I wouldn't take ownership of that decision. Blame it on something. PMS, lack of sleep. Or alcohol." Edie raised her glass and took a swig, feeling the warm burn inside her.

"I should have gone to the salon," Patience moaned, and Edie proceeded to give her a rundown of what she missed.

"Jane Eyre was a pansy. Mr. Rochester was a dickwad and Jane should have never had faith in a man who kept a crazy wife in the attic." Realizing that she might sound bitter, Edie laughed.

"You're okay?" asked Wanda, who might have noticed the tremors in Edie's laughter. Reading the concern on Wanda's face, Edie rolled her eyes, because Edie was the role model for these women. The epitome of a smart, foot-loose woman who would live her life on her own terms, finding happiness where she could before dancing off to some new adventure. Never staying too long, lest she ended up staring wistfully at an empty doorway.

Edie kept her eyes firmly on her friends. "Are you kidding? I'm fine."

"Me, too," announced Patience.

"Me, three," added Wanda.

Edie didn't dare ask why Patience and Wanda were here with her, what warning signs they'd noticed that Edie had overlooked. However, these were her friends, there in her time of need, and although as a rule, Edie avoided having times of need, she wasn't so sure that avoiding something actually eliminated the existence of something. Apparently, when nursing a bruised heart as a well as a cherry-topped coconut drink, she lapsed into the philosophical, which was a helluva lot more comforting than a lot of other things.

Slowly, the pain in her heart numbed and Edie looked at Patience and Wanda and smiled in what some might term a vulnerable, teary manner, which wasn't a good look for a role model.

"Thanks," Edie said quietly, not exactly wanting to be heard. It might imply that she was unhappy and as dippy as the next female, and frankly, considering her friends' own precarious strength of will, they didn't need to be disillusioned with the truth.

Apparently Wanda had supersonic hearing, or perhaps Edie had intended to be heard. "Hell, Edie, how many times have you kicked us back on our feet? Did you think we wouldn't return the favor?"

Edie laughed, but no, Edie hadn't thought they would return the favor, and just the thought of it was getting her all misty again.

Patience slammed back her drink, and then pulled Edie and Wanda to their feet. "Let's sing," she pronounced, sounding completely sober, yet scarily insane. "Let's get up there and prove to everybody that we're fine. Fine-looking, fine-feeling, fine-hearted females who…" She trailed off, looking disappointed. "I ran out of *F* words."

Wanda bust out laughing. "We're not singing."

"Come on? Are we a bunch of pansies?" Patience asked.

"Yes," muttered Edie.

Patience made a fist and pumped it in the air. "No, we are strong. We are invincible."

"I think she's drunk," Wanda pronounced.

"I think you're chicken," Patience shot back, meeting Edie's eyes with a familiar, diabolical, devil-may-care gleam.

Then, Wanda looked at Edie with those "she's right" eyes, and Edie squirmed because she wasn't a singer. She liked to sit back and have a good time, knowing that she would never put anything important on the line, but there was Patience, staring at her, expecting her to put something important on their line. The worst thing was the doubt in Wanda's face. She didn't think that Edie would.

"You are going to make me do this?"

"Jane Eyre wouldn't," stated Wanda.

Now, Edie knew that Wanda knew that was the red flag to the bull, the smell of blood to the shark, the bugle call for every army that had ever marched off to their death.

However, Edie was neither shark nor bull nor soldier. "Don't compare me to her," she said, putting her hands on hips.

"If the pinched-toe shoes fit," mocked Patience.

Edie glared. "I don't sing," she protested, and her own words echoed back in her head: Bricks don't sing, either. Don't be a brick.

"It doesn't matter. I don't bowl," said Patience, whose confidence was now growing in leaps and bounds and she was fast becoming a royal pain in the butt.

"Fine," answered Edie, as Wanda dragged her up on stage. "But I'm not going to sing."

"Follow my moves," whispered Patience, pulling the mike off the stand and waving it at the audience. "I win the open mike night at my local all the time."

"Do we have to do this?" pleaded Edie, just as Patience held out a hand and then burst forth with those unforgettable words...

"Stop, in the name of love!"

Oh, god.

"Put on your big-girl panties," teased Wanda.

And Edie knew that she was well and truly beaten.

The audience began to clap, the skeevy kid ogled and leered and Edie made a mockery of background dancers everywhere. "I hate this," she whispered through tightly clenched teeth.

"Think it oh-oh-oh-over," sang Wanda. "Go with it. Lighten up. Be free from the rigid confines of someone else's expectations."

"Why do you listen to me?" she asked. When Wanda

poked her in the side, she turned sideways to the audience and sang. "Baby, baby. Oh, oh..."

"You're smarter than you know, Edie."

Smarter? No. Not smarter, because as they sang—slightly off-key—and looked more than a little silly, Edie began to smile, no longer pretending to. She liked the non-judgey atmosphere of the crowd, but no matter the warmth inside her, no matter that her friends stood beside her, when no one was looking, her eyes still strayed to the door.

Foolishly waiting.

Idiot.

_10_

TYLER'S EYES CRACKED OPEN, the first rays of sunlight peeking through sterile white blinds. Hospital blinds. He reached out, found scratchy hospital sheet, and sighed. Memories from this afternoon's surgery flooded his mind. Especially the moment when he had taken the lead to restart the prime minister's heart and heard the glorious sound of sinus rhythm.

Max Lockwood was screwed.

With a wide yawn, Tyler pulled himself upright and grinned.

Nothing like the smell of victory in the morning.

Nothing like a hot date tonight.

He checked his watch and it was at that precise instant, as he was still basking in the glow of success, that Tyler realized the surgery had lasted over twenty-four hours. Today wasn't Monday. It was Tuesday. On Monday, he'd had a date with Edie.

Yesterday.

Shit.

Still not panicked, he'd checked his phone, expecting a voice mail, a text message, something to indicate that Tyler was an irresponsible brick, but there was nothing and he frowned, because Tyler deserved a snippy text message, or an angry voice mail, or something.

Anything.

Nothing.

Quickly, he shrugged into his jacket, brushing out the wrinkles. For a second, he took a hard look in the mirror, uncomfortable with the sloppy hair, the glittering professional ambition in his eyes. It had been a long time since Tyler had disappointed anyone. Not since he was a kid, and it was a behavior that he'd ruthlessly eliminated from his life. So what was a man supposed to do when he messed up? These were the sorts of things that Edie was supposed to teach him. If she didn't kill him first.

He'd buy some flowers—no, no flowers for Edie.

A card? Nope.

Edie would expect him to use his charm and sincerity. A moving plea of emotional candor.

God almighty, Tyler was screwed.

THERE WERE UPSIDES TO an honest, hard-working, hands-dirty vocation. When a girl was bummed, it was possible to bury her worries in food, grime, dishwater, or sometimes a gross brown mixture of all three.

On Tuesday morning, Edie had zoomed from sink to stove to office to tables to cashier and then back to the sink. It wasn't the life she would have chosen when she was a kid, but now, Edie was glad she had rethought her earlier career choices of astronaut and computer hacker, neither of which had customers like Mrs. Kohner, who liked her eggs runny and her toast charcoal-black. Nor would she have met women like Patience or Wanda or Khandi. Women who had her back.

The lunch rush had just finished when Patience skidded into the kitchen. "Are you sitting down?" she asked, then pushed Edie to a stool. "You should sit down."

"Is there something wrong?" Edie asked cautiously, because frankly, she didn't want to deal with any more wrongs at the moment. Bacon grease was about the biggest problem she wanted to handle at the moment.

"It's your father. He's at table three. I never knew your father, but you know, you have his eyes. They're really pretty. Sort of tawny."

"Dad's here?" Yes, he had said he might show up, but politicians promised balanced budgets, dietetic food products promised great taste and weathermen promised that it wouldn't rain.

"Up front. Go on. He looks like he's in a hurry."

"Sure," said Edie, and disbelieving, she walked through the diner just to the same.

"Dad? You're here?"

His smile was charming and sheepish and completely sure that she would forgive him. "I know. It's the end times."

"Something like that," she murmured, sliding into the booth across the table from him, fighting the instinctive urge to forgive him.

"I owe you an apology," her father started, but Edie cut him off.

"No, you don't. An apology would mean that my expectations were not met. You meet my expectations on a daily basis, Dad."

He clasped his hand to his chest. "Ouch. I can see you handle knives as well as your old man."

"Not nearly as heroically. You save lives with yours. I merely toss them out and see where they land."

Her father sighed. "Are you going to let me apologize?"

Edie agreed.

"I know I'm not the dad you want. I know I'm not the dad you need, but I'm the only dad you've got. Someday

I will retire, and then we'll have time for those father-daughter chats that I always wanted to have."

Oh, yes, the myth of the perfect family. Edie glanced out the window and noted that it looked like rain. "Retirement? Dad, you're approaching seventy. I think your golden years are going to be spent hunched over an operating table, your instruments not trembling at all."

Her father held out his hands, steady and firm. "They are holding up well, aren't they? Not any of the distal tremors that Les Harbinger has."

"He doesn't have anything on you, and you know it."

"True. Did I tell you about the surgery yesterday? A prime minister. His heart stopped twice."

Whenever her father talked about his work, his face would light up with drama and pride, and Edie leaned forward because everyone always listened intently when the tales of the table began. "Did you save him?"

"No. Some other young hotshot with dreams of surgical grandeur."

"You're jealous," she teased, pleasantly surprised that her father would admit it.

"Maybe," he hedged, still not admitting it, but almost.

It was the first time she had seen the sad awareness in his eyes. Medical science did much to save life, prolong life, but in the end, the body and the mind were destined for weakness.

"Do you *want* to retire?" she asked, not so discreetly, but he seemed to be more approachable today, less luminary, and more like a dad. It was nice, and thus, she could ask these sorts of impertinent questions that regular daughters would ask.

Her father chuckled. "Retire? Nah. Your mother would kill me. I'd be doddering around the house, complaining about this, correcting that, and after a week, you'd find us lying on the floor in a pool of blood. And then you'd be all alone."

She quirked a brow. "Thinking of me? Is that it?"

"Always. I'm not here a lot, Edie Ma Didi, but I think of you all the time. You and Clarice." He picked up her hand, curling his fingers around hers, resting it on the cut and gouged Formica tabletop.

The most useful of objects often bore the most scars. "Don't make me cry, Dad."

"You don't cry. You're tough. You're strong. You're invincible."

"I could be vincible and you'd never know," she told him, not completely a joke.

Her father missed it, or perhaps he chose to ignore it. "You want to go see a movie? Surgery's been rescheduled."

"Seriously? You're off this afternoon?"

He looked sheepish. "No, I have a consult in half an hour."

Edie laughed, feeling herself being swayed to the dark side. It was like that with her father. A few minutes in his company, and she was willing to forget all prior bad acts.

"Let's make a plan. A real plan. What would you like to do? You always wanted us to go to the zoo. We could do the zoo. Next week? Wednesday."

"I'm twenty-eight, Dad. I've been to the zoo."

He looked at her, offended. "Not with me."

"You've never been?"

"Not with you."

"Next Wednesday?" Edie repeated, but she didn't have to write it down. "It's a date. Thanks for stopping by."

"I'll do it more often."

"Right," she mocked, but when their eyes met, she couldn't help but wink. That was the allure of her father. He lived in a different universe, occupied not with celebrities or politicians, but a place where true superheroes lived.

And they always lived alone.

TYLER'S FIRST INDICATION as to the full extent of his trouble was the glare from Patience. He winced and found a booth near the window. The diner was busy for a Tuesday, but there was no sign of Edie.

Not that he could blame her.

There were men who didn't accept their mistakes, but Tyler took his own lumps.

Although if it hadn't been for Max...

Wanda tossed a menu in his general direction, and Tyler smiled cautiously. "What's good today?"

"Fried testicles," she snapped.

Beneath the table his hand went protectively to his crotch. "Is Edie here?"

"Why do you care?"

"I want to apologize."

"Were you dead? You don't look dead. You look very healthy. A little rough around the edges. Slept in your clothes? Out whoring?"

It was obvious—even to a less perceptive mind—that a simple apology wasn't going to fix this. If he threw himself in front of a bus, would that help? He noted Wanda's artic gaze.

Nope. The bus wouldn't help, either. "I need to talk to Edie and apologize."

Wanda popped her gum and then shrugged. "Let me see if she's here. Don't know, though. Sometimes she's in. Sometimes she's out. Sometimes she's out for a long time. In fact, sometimes she's out until hell freezes over, if you take my meaning."

"Please?"

"Practice that begging, mister. You're going to need it."

If Tyler were a smarter man, he would leave now, but then he caught sight of Edie coming his way. Her eyes were cool, dismissive, unforgiving, as if he didn't exist.

He needed to exist in Edie's world because she knew him in ways no one else did. Edie was a reminder of all the good things that his father had slowly dissected from him.

Wanda's words echoed in his head. *Until hell freezes over.*

Yes, she was currently mad as hell. And yes, hell would have to freeze first.

So would he wait that long?

For her? Hell, yes.

EDIE NEVER LIKED confrontations, or at least, the meaningful kind. A confrontation meant that interests were vested, and in the end, there would be one winner, and one loser. Edie didn't like to lose, but right now there was a hole in her gut, much like a loser's would feel.

Or so she'd been told.

After skimming damp palms over faded jeans, she sat down at Tyler's table.

"I'm sorry," Tyler said.

She wished he were a little more chipper like her dad had been because then it would be easier to write him off. Apologies were coming a dime a dozen today, but still they were merely words.

Edie waved an easy-breezy hand, indicating a lack of pain or hurt or disappointment or any sort of emotional connection at all. "Don't worry. Hey. You were busy."

"I can explain," he offered, his eyes betraying what looked to be actual regret.

"No need." After all, it wasn't as if she wasn't dying to hear his excuse. She'd known him for next-to-no time, and there was no way that she would let herself *hurt* from such a cheap, meaningless relationship. In fact, because she was not hurt, she grinned and leaned her elbows on the table. "Let's just write it off as just one of those things, and build a bridge. I'm a fan of bridges. What about you?"

"Edie—" he began in that silky, earnest voice of his, and she let the sound wash over her, softening her anger.

Quickly she cut him off before she softened even more. "Hey, you're an adult. I'm an adult. It's not like you have to check in with me, and it wasn't even a big deal. Last night, we had a ladies' night, drinking, carousing, doing all those fun, lady things. Now that I think about it—because I haven't up until now—you probably would have been in the way."

Edie paused, giving him an opportunity to explain. Although she hoped that her face didn't say, "I'll give you another chance." She suspected that it did, because slowly, awkwardly, he began to tell her.

"I was at work, doing this big project, and I lost track of time...and you don't deserve that."

"Deserve what?" she scoffed, doing more easy-breezy hands, and keeping the smile plastered firmly on her face. It was harder than it looked.

"I screwed up, and I should have called, but then..." He shoved a hand through his hair and swore. "I don't abandon my obligations."

For the first time, she let a hint of anger creep into her voice. "I'm not an obligation."

Tyler whacked himself on the head, not nearly as hard as she would have, but then he looked at her, and he seemed so miserable that if he hadn't stood her up last night, she might have reached out to comfort him. "Can I make this up to you?"

Edie laughed. "Nothing to make up. Maybe in Texas you guys are all, 'Oh, little lady needs some TLC because she might get trampled,' but this is New York, lover. We don't expect anything from our men at all."

That at least was true. New York was a jungle where only the strongest survived. In the movies, the male/female dynamic always seemed so easy, and she'd heard rumors that other cities weren't so bloodthirsty, but Edie didn't believe it. The male species was hardwired to dominate. The female was hardwired to submit.

Winners and losers. Always.

"Can I take you out this afternoon? Lunch? Show? Public flogging at my hotel?"

His mouth twisted nervously, and she almost felt his pain. Edie covered a hand over her face and coughed because empathy implied that someone mattered and that really wasn't necessary. Yes, she wanted to go with him, yes, her legs were already poised in the locked and upright position to do that very thing, but Edie had work to do here. She had obligations to her friends, and to herself. She took them as seriously as he did.

Or, at least, she was starting to now.

"Please. Before now, I really truly sucked at these things, and I didn't care. I still do suck at this, Edie. But now I care."

Edie glanced down at the menu between them and slowly, cautiously, she looked up and met his eyes. Slowly, cautiously, she nodded. "Meet me here tonight," she instructed.

"You know I was kidding about the flogging at the hotel?"

For the first time that afternoon, Tyler smiled at her, and Edie smiled in response.

"Lighten up, Hart," she told him, reaching out to touch his hand, a buddy sort of hit rather than a gentle caress, but her fingers lingered. Hopefully he didn't notice.

He grabbed her fingers, held them there and nodded once. "Eight?"

"Make it nine," she instructed. "Wanda has an exam tomorrow and I need to cover for her so she can pass. Speaking of, I need to get back to it. Books to balance, food to cook, people to feed. Lots of hungry people." Thankfully, the diner looked busy, and the lies didn't seem as obvious as they felt.

"See you then," he said, squeezing her hand before letting go.

Edie slid away, out of reach of the unwavering eyes, and escaped to the kitchen. There was an anticipatory spring in her step and a flutter of hope in her heart that was absolutely not from being happy.

Why had he come back? Her life would have been so much easier if Tyler Hart had simply disappeared forever.

11

THEY WERE HALFWAY DOWN the steps to the 34th Street subway station, when Tyler stopped what he knew was a disaster in the making. "Do you really have your heart set on Rollerblading?" he asked carefully, as he dodged the crowd and worked his way back up the stairs, pulling Edie behind him.

"My heart is set on nothing. Why?" she asked.

"I'd like to do something where conversation is possible. I'm not very good at conversation, so it would be like part of a lesson. You promised," he reminded her.

"You can talk while Rollerblading," Edie pointed out.

Tyler moved her out of the way of a man carrying his bike—to the subway. New York was a strange and curious place. Down below, in the bowels of the earth, Tyler could hear the next rumbling crowd moving up toward them.

"You can't talk while Rollerblading. That's yelling," Tyler yelled as people spilled out around them. "I don't like to yell."

Edie stood fast. "People don't converse in New York," she yelled.

People swelled around them. For a minute she disappeared in the sea of faces, but she was still holding his hand. A good thing. Eventually, the crowd thinned out and Tyler took his shot and tugged her closer.

She was arguing with him but they were a step away from doing something other than Rollerblading. Yes. It was definitely progress.

"So where are we going?" she asked him.

And there, a beacon in blue and white, was the answer.

Edie noticed the direction of his gaze and gasped in horror. "The Empire State Building? It's hot, the lines are long and—"

"You hate it?"

She met his eyes, and Tyler assumed his most beseeching, puppy-dog expression. It wasn't a look he did well, but apparently it was enough. Edie smiled. "If you have your heart set on going, we'll go."

TURNED OUT THE OBSERVATION deck was closed due to repairs. While Edie spent the next ten minutes, charming, arguing, bribing the lady at the desk, Tyler noticed the security guard, a thin, older man with still-sharp eyes that were assessing Tyler as if he knew him.

As the guard approached, Tyler realized why the security guard knew him. His wife had been the CABG that Dr. Keating had performed on Monday. Hoffman? *Howard?*

"Dr. Hart," the guard was saying. "Charlie Heeney. My wife…"

Tyler interrupted before the man could divulge Tyler's actual career choice to Edie. As a medical professional, he understood the importance of not saying too much too soon, revealing information in direct proportion to the listener's ability to calmly process said information.

In Tyler's opinion, he'd just dodged one bullet, getting Edie to come out with him tonight after last night's screwup, before having to dodge another. He needed a break. Tyler wasn't used to a lot of what did Edie call it? TLC. Yes, that's what it was.

Cynthia wasn't nearly as hands-on as Edie was, and Tyler was discovering that hands-on had a lot of things going for it, namely plenty of lewd touching, but it was hard work, as well.

Tyler clasped the man in a friendly gesture, before pitching his voice low. "She's doing okay?"

"Up and about and giving me orders, and I'm thinking I wouldn't mind having her in the hospital for an extra day or two," the guard complained, but then he rubbed his face. "Mother of God, I thought I'd never hear her give me orders again."

Tyler kept an eye on Edie, who was laughing with the ticket agent, clearly still determined to get them upstairs. "Can you do me a favor?"

"You're wanting to go to the top, are you? I'd be honored to give you a lift. My humble way of saying thanks."

"That'd be great, but don't mention the surgery. My friend's funny that way. She's been trying to bribe the agent into getting us up there, and I didn't have the heart to tell her that it was a waste of time. She loves to get her way."

"Mrs. Heeney's just the same. No worries," Charlie reassured him. "It's a hard row to hoe, keeping a woman happy, day in, day out. A man might think they'd have a clue of the sacrifices we make, but the truth is, I don't think they know."

Tyler looked over at Edie and smiled. "No, they have no idea."

The security guard strolled toward the reception desk. "Janet, is there some problem?"

"This couple wants to go to the top, but I told her no can do. Construction."

Heeney stuck his hands in his pockets and rocked back on his heels, as if considering the matter. "Well, construction hasn't started yet, don't even think they've brought there tools or supplies. And I'm thinking it's hard finding a time when you're both free to come back."

On cue, Tyler and Edie nodded apologetically. Heeney jangled his keys and returned their nod. "Janet, I was wanting to take a last look around. I'll take care of this."

As he waved them on to the elevator, Edie grinned and grabbed Tyler's hand, and the security guard gave him a wink. Once they arrived on the roof, Edie led Tyler over to the south observation deck and for a few minutes, they were silent, taking in the view. It was a different world, a world of new opportunities that Taylor wanted to explore. To conquer.

"It's not Houston, I'll give you that."

Edie kept her eyes locked on the city. "My father showed up at the diner today."

He noted her careful stillness and asked, "How did it go?"

She was silent, then she looked at him and frowned. "Nice. Normal. Very strange."

Tyler winced at the words. Frank Hart had kept his son from caring, and Dr. Higgins made his daughter care too much. Tyler didn't like lying to her about his profession, but he wasn't sure exactly how to tell her, either.

"Would you be happy if your father was an ordinary eight-to-fiver? Punching a clock, and coming home to complain about his boss?" Tyler hoped her answer would be no.

"I didn't used to want that. I used to think my father was the greatest man in the world."

"And now?"

Her smile was more than a little sad. "He's still the greatest man in the world. When you're a kid, you don't worry about connecting to your parents—they're like gods. But when you're an adult, you realize that gods are unreachable, matter how high you fly, no matter how fast you run." Then she laughed at herself and he took her hand and she held it tightly. "I don't mean to be depressing. How was the museum? What's the day-to-day like? I should go there and see a day in the life of a curator."

"You wouldn't like it, trust me. Not enough excitement for you."

Edie breathed in deeply, taking in all the hopes and dreams that lay just out of her reach. "I don't want to slow down. Not ever."

"Never is an absolute. Absolutes are always wrong."

"But there's so much to do. So many people to talk to, to learn from. So many topics. So many worlds. How can you stop a top from spinning?"

The words said one thing, the worried tone implied another.

"Eventually it falls over." He leaned over the side. "Hopefully not off the Empire State Building."

Edie looked at him. "You like being settled, don't you?"

Tyler frowned. "I've never thought of myself as the settled type before."

"You are."

"I don't think so."

"You don't flit. You pick a spot and stay there. You're no flake."

"Well, no, but it's not very flattering to think of yourself as the solitary signpost at the end of the woods. There's nothing wrong with wanting to be Times Square."

Edie motioned toward the flash of neon. "Sometimes all those lights can burn your retinas. Grounded is good. The world needs gravity, or else we'd all be floating in space."

"I'm gravity?"

"You have gravitas. From the Latin word for weight-iness."

Tyler considered that for a minute. "Heroic virtue or character flaw?"

"Both."

"So when do we get to dissect you?" he asked. Tyler simply was who he was.

"This isn't about quid pro quo. You're all surface, all smooth waters, but nobody gets to see what's underneath," said the woman who ran in place at a thousand miles per hour. However, Tyler was smart enough not to point that out.

"You want to see what's underneath? I'll show you what's underneath."

"Do not think that your smarmy double entendres will divert me from the truth."

"I'll consider myself warned. Do you want to eat? I'm hungry."

"How about dessert?" she asked him with an impish smile, dimples flashing. Instantly his mind moved on to bigger and better things. Getting naked. Feeling her body locked against his. Her mouth...

"I love dessert," he said, getting hungrier by the second. But not for food. Not anymore.

"Great, I know this French place on Twenty-Fourth Street. The pastries are to die for."

He blinked, wondering why women weren't as simple as men. "Pastries? Were we talking about pastries? I wasn't talking about pastries. "

She kissed him soft and sweet, which of course turned him on even more.

Sadly, he shook his head. "Pastries it is."

THE BISTRO WAS SMALL. Eight tables only, wooden floors, glass counters filled with very high-fat foods that kept Tyler in business. At first, he wanted to confess his lie before she ordered, but then the waiter had been too fast, and then he wanted to tell her before the desserts arrived, but he couldn't find the right words, and now the plates were in front of them, and Tyler knew he had run out of excuses.

It was time.

"You should know something. I'm a doctor."

"I know that."

"M.D."

"Oh," she said, and then casually continued to drizzle hot fudge over her berries.

Tyler waited silently, expecting the outburst, but the outburst never came. "I expected this to be a bigger issue."

"Why?" she asked, looking at him as if he was out of his mind, but the sparkle in her eyes was gone.

"*Why?* Because you don't like doctors."

"I'm sure I said that, but you don't need to take everything I say at face value," she said, and continued to attack her dessert.

"Anyway, I wanted you to know."

"Sure." Another mouthful of dessert later, she frowned at her phone. "Minor emergency. Give me a sec," she said, then she took off for the back.

THERE WAS AN EXIT IN the alley, and Edie told the busboy that she had a family emergency and needed to leave. The tears in her eyes added to the effect. It would have been nice if that was acting, too.

A doctor.

If she thought about this rationally, she knew there were worse men in the world. There were serial killers and conceited egomaniacs who only talked about themselves. There were Wall Street tycoons who lived for gold cards and Ferraris.

Rationally she knew that a woman would have to be nuts to hate the medical profession, and a selfish nut at that.

Rationally, Edie didn't want to be a selfish nut, but her stomach was starting to cramp and she had sat alone in a karaoke bar, convinced that Tyler was...

Different.

Not a big deal, not a big deal, she repeated in her head, but her feet had other ideas, and in less than ten minutes she was standing in her apartment, having left Dr. Tyler Hart in a universe far, far away.

IT TOOK TYLER A GOOD twenty minutes before he realized that Edie had left the building. Normally, he wasn't so dense, and he'd like to blame it on lack of sleep, or distractions, or excitement over possibly working long-term with Dr. Keating. None of which were applicable.

If the truth had bothered her, which he knew it would, she should have admitted it, and they could have discussed it, after which, she would have left.

Tyler considered the scenario from every direction and they all ended the same way.

Edie out the door.

He should leave her alone. They had a fly-by-night relationship of little more than sex and he had gotten caught up in the vortex of who Edie Higgins was. Tyler should have been able to do what he always did. Turn the page. Move on.

Nope.

Tyler paid the check, made a quick phone call and then hailed a cab, nearly getting run over in the process. He yelled at the driver, and when he'd realized that he'd done it, he started to laugh.

For better or worse, she'd left her mark. And for the second time in twenty-four hours he had to beg, plead, and grovel to get her back. He'd done it once, he could do it twice.

Not too shabby for an emotional brick if he did say so himself.

HER BUZZER RANG SOONER than she'd expected.

"What do you need?" she asked.

"You left."

"Sorry," she said, and rang off.

The buzzer rang again.

"Who is this?"

"Tyler."

"Sorry," she said, and rang off.

Once again, the buzzer sounded.

She pounded at the button. "What?"

"If you actually didn't want to talk to me, you wouldn't be answering the bell."

"Good night, Tyler."

"I'll sing—"

And then she heard it. Eight stories below, a doctor, originally from Texas, was singing like a dying animal.

Reluctantly she buzzed him up.

He stood in her doorway in neat suit, meticulous Windsor knot and a stubborn gleam in his eyes. "You left."

She nodded once, keeping safe distance between them. She was onto his act now, playing the part of the helpless, clueless, buttoned-up man. Buried underneath all that respectability was the shifty heart of the devil.

"You said it didn't bother you. If it bothered you, why didn't you tell me?"

She shrugged, as if it didn't bother her, and Tyler narrowed his eyes.

"Can we talk?" he asked.

"Go ahead."

"Inside?"

She stared into the narrow passage with its muted gray carpet and bright wallpapered walls. "I like the hallway."

"Please," he said.

She heaved an exaggerated sigh.

Once inside her small apartment, he didn't bother to look around, didn't bother to sit. Every inch of him, every delicious inch of him was focused on her.

"I'm sorry. I didn't mean to lie."

"No big deal."

"Don't lie."

At that, she raised her brows. "Why? You own the trademark on that one?"

"I told you."

"After the fact," she reminded him. "After you had stood me up," she added, because the lie on its own, well, she couldn't throw stones, but he knew her feelings on doctors. He knew why she didn't get all woo-woo over the workaholic lifestyle, and he still, *still* ended up leaving her high and dry.

"Yes. That was wrong, too," he admitted.

"So, I don't see why you're here. Go back to the hospital, Tyler. All this stress will earn you an ulcer, or raise your blood pressure. Oh, but you're a doctor, so I guess it doesn't matter. What specialty?"

"Cardio," he answered through gritted teeth.

She laughed. "I should have guessed. Are you at St. Agnes?"

"Yes," he answered, because, of course, all great, dedicated doctors worked there, and yes, Dr. Tyler Hart would be one of those. No slacker here. No, siree.

"It's a great hospital. Lots of experimental procedures, lots of research dollars, lots of celebrity patients. You heard that prime minister was there?"

"I know."

"You were the hotshot doc who saved him?"

She saw a flush rise on his cheeks.

He had stood her up because he had been saving the prime minister's life. This great, noble act should have made her feel better, instead, it only made her want to cry. "Why are you here?"

"Because I do not do things like this. I do not stand up women. I do not tell lies. I am responsible, I am intelligent. I am a good person."

Yes, he was a good person. He was a great person. Unfortunately, she wasn't that strong, and the pain was too much.

"We had sex, Tyler. It was good. It was fun. Go do your doctor thing and don't worry about me, will you?"

"You're supposed to know how to do these things."

"What things?"

"The emotional crap."

"I can't do the emotional crap. Don't be a brick, Tyler. Not now. I suck at the emotional crap. I love to tell everyone else what to do because what you can't do, you teach, right?"

"You can do this," he told her.

"Maybe, but I won't. It hurts, Tyler. I don't want to hurt."

"I like you. Is that so difficult to understand?"

"It's the sex. It confuses people. You're too intelligent to be confused."

"I'm not confused," he insisted, sounding not even remotely confused.

Edie lifted her hands in frustration. "Do you want the sex?"

"Yes. No. I don't care."

She stared at him, letting her silence make her point.

"I'm not," he insisted.

"What?"

"Confused," he stated very firmly. "We can do this."

"Why are you in the city, Tyler? Really? The truth."

He stuck his hands in his pockets, his jaw tight with tension. "The ACT/Keating Endowment Award."

"You won it?"

"No, I'm one of the candidates for it. It's a two-month fellowship, and then the decision will be made about who stays on to work with Dr. Keating for another two years. It's a life-changing opportunity."

"How many other candidates are there?"

"Two hundred."

"How do they decide who gets this great and glorious honor?"

"Dr. Keating picks someone."

"The sharpest, the hardest working, the most creative, the biggest overachiever in the bunch?"

"Something like that."

"And you want this fellowship, don't you? You want it bad, don't you, Tyler?"

"I'm going to win."

"Putting in all the hours, all the doc-talk, all the suck-up, all the research that winning entails."

"Whatever it takes."

"Do you see why I have concerns? Do you see why I am skeptical that you will have two minutes, much less ten minutes, much less ten days in the next two months. When exactly were we supposed to see each other? How many times will I be left waiting alone? How many promises would you need to break?"

"None. Some."

"No. You can't do everything, Tyler. You can't be everything to everyone. You want to be Dr. Hart, you go ahead, but you can't be Perfect Man, too."

"We could try?" He tried to reach out to her, but she backed away.

"No."

"All right. Then we do it your way. No promises. No dates. Sex. You said that's all you wanted because you don't do relationships." He used quote fingers, just in case she missed the sarcasm in his voice. "If we're not involved, then it shouldn't matter if I'm a doc, right?"

The devil was crafty, sly and stubborn.

"I don't like this."

"Why? Are you worried that you'd get involved with a surgeon?"

She was already involved. She knew it. He knew it. It was a big part of the problem. She put up her chin. "I'm not worried."

"Prove it. Put up or shut up, Edie."

"Very crude, don't you think?"

"Hey, it's New York."

Edie pulled her shirt over her head, and whipped off the rest of her clothes, and then stood there, naked and defiant. Of course, since he was a doc, naked meant nothing to him.

The doc's eyes flared. "Don't do this," he warned, but Edie knew when she had the devil by the tail.

"I thought we had decided we were going to do this," she said, hands on hips. "Put up or shut up, Tyler."

Put up, it was. He had her flat on her back, on the floor, and didn't bother with his clothes. She heard the rasp of a zip, the rip of the condom wrapper and the heavy pant of her own breathing, but then he was between her legs, filling her, killing her, and it was a glorious pain.

"I don't like this," he protested, even as his body drove in for more.

"I can...tell," she managed to say, her fingers twisting at his buttons and knots. The man had too many clothes, she needed to touch...*skin*. There. Her hands found the strong arch of his buttocks, and she held tight, absorbing each thrust, loving this, needing this.

Needing him.

He found her mouth, and she tasted coffee and lust and the same furious need as her own. His tongue mated with the fast rhythm of his cock, and her hips lifted higher, wanting more. This was Edie's crime. She always wanted more.

He gave her more. Over and over. He rode her until she forgot her anger, forgot her fears and forgot her own name. It was the very best sort of sex. Driven by arguments unfinished, words left unsaid. He pulled her on top, his chest heaving, his shirt half undone and his tie like a noose. Only the serious eyes belonged to Dr. Tyler Hart. Edie didn't want to get trapped there, but he was sneaky and sly. His hips slowed their pace, his fingers trailed over her breasts, and she arched into him, meeting him halfway.

He opened his mouth to speak, and she covered it with her own. It was meant to be a sexy kiss, a fuck-me kiss, as her fingers slid into his hair, locking him to her.

She and Tyler stayed there for a long time, entangled on the floor. Sometimes she slept, sometimes she woke to find him inside her, but each time he tried to speak, she shushed him with a kiss. She didn't want promises. Promises, just like hearts, were meant to be broken.

12

FRIDAY AFTERNOON'S SURGERY was a double valve replacement for a seventy-year-old class IV patient. The E.R. had shipped her up to surgery with a 25-percent ejection fraction, and a blood pressure in the danger zone. Tyler seated the valves, Max tied the purse strings and after one hundred and seventy-nine minutes, Dr. Keating pronounced the operation a success and went out to dinner with Max.

Not that Tyler was too concerned, since he had a date with Edie tonight. Technically, it was not a date, because he could not call it a date. Edie would only refer to it as his booty call, which sounded about as sexually titillating as a hygiene textbook. However, Tyler had his own ideas, and yes, booty was involved, but before he got her naked, he was going to take her to the museum. There were mummies and other ancient artifacts, and Tyler was very proud that he'd even thought of it. Yes, dead bodies did hearken back to an earlier, simpler time in their relationship when he was masquerading as a museum curator, but by visiting the actual museum, not only did it prove to her that they could move past his prior mistake, but it also demonstrated that he remembered all the things she had told him. Elegant, yet effective. Certainly he was no Dr. Romeo, but he was catching on.

When he was halfway to his locker room, he spotted Charlie Heeney sitting on one of the brown standard-issued couches.

"Mr. Heeney?"

"Dr. Hart," Charlie said, rising slowly to his feet.

"Why are you here? Is it Eileen? No one paged me."

"The nurse told us you were in surgery and Mrs. Heeney wasn't of a mind to worry you. Yesterday her chest was paining her and she didn't say a word, but this morning, after she had her coffee, she felt a twinge and I told her we were coming here straight away. No arguments, no complaints." He heaved a tired sigh. "Apparently it was nothing but last night's stew."

"I could take a look," Tyler offered, but Charlie held up a hand.

"No need to bother with bad stew. Go be with your lady friend."

"I will. Page me if it happens again."

Charlie smiled. "It won't. Tomorrow my daughter is cooking for us." He patted his chest. "She goes easier on the garlic than Mrs. Heeney."

After he'd changed into a clean suit, Tyler got a page, sending him to the pavilion. He frowned, not sure why someone would want him there. The pavilion was a large room with three separate cafeteria areas, a lounge area on the far side of the room with stuffed chairs and newspapers and several flat-screen televisions worthy of a sports bar. Back in the corner, Tyler spied a cowboy hat and shook his head.

God, New Yorkers really needed to learn something.

The hat turned, and Tyler spotted the familiar face underneath the hat.

Austen.

Cheerfully Austen waved, and Tyler glowered in return. If he were a colder man, he would abandon his brother, but right then, Tyler was more concerned about the innocent medical staff at St. Agnes. His brother had three women surrounding him, three women who had no idea of the damage that Austen Hart could do.

No, Tyler would need to save them.

Damn it.

"Hello, Austen."

Austen jumped up and slapped him on the back like long-lost family.

"Ladies, this is the famous Dr. Tyler Hart. He's the one I've been telling you about. Ty, say hello to your fans."

Famous? Tyler shot Austen a dark look and then managed a half smile for the women. "I'm just out of surgery, and haven't seen my brother in a few weeks, so you'll have to pardon us for a few minutes."

Quickly Tyler shoved his brother down in his chair and then took an open seat across from him, since the ones immediately adjacent were occupied by Emma Sanderson, a nurse in pink scrubs, and another woman in a business suit.

"Isn't he modest?" Austen said with a grin, but the women stood up, about to leave them to blessed privacy, where Tyler could castrate his brother without witnesses.

As Sanderson was about to leave, Austen caught her by the arm. "Emma, we're still on for tonight? You and Julie? Tyler needs a night out to lift his spirits. Look at that face." Austen pointed at Tyler. "He needs something to cheer him up."

After the women left, Tyler rounded on his brother.

"What the hell was that about?"

"We have a double date for tonight. Nurse Sanderson was fascinated by your sabbatical to Kenya, and Nurse

Goodnight liked the scar on my neck. I thought you'd be happy that I didn't stick you with the shallow one."

Tyler shoved his hand through his hair. "What if I don't want to go on a date?"

"After I went to all this work to help you out?" Austen told him, looking hurt and betrayed.

"What work?" asked Tyler, not fooled by the acting skills of a lobbyist. "It probably took you all of an hour."

"Fifteen minutes. You can thank me later. It'll be fun."

Austen flicked at finger at the brim of his hat, much like a man who wore a hat every day. Austen did not wear a cowboy hat every day, but he knew enough to fool people. Much like he fooled women into believing that he understood them, much like he fooled women into believing that he was actually responding to their deeply hidden emotional truths. Sometimes Tyler really wanted to punch his brother, but then he'd probably break a bone, and Tyler would have to fix it because Austen would expect it, and Tyler was responsible. It would only be one more thing that Austen could hold over Tyler's head.

"Sure, you'll hate it," Austen said, "and you hate spinach, too, but you know it's good for you, so you force yourself to eat it, and look at spinach now. People are sticking it in everything and calling it fancy names. Think of tonight as spinach."

For a second Tyler closed his eyes, hoping this was a bad dream, but no, when he opened his eyes, Austen was still there. "Why didn't you tell me you were coming?"

"I did."

"No, you didn't. I told you I didn't want you here. That's how we left it."

"You sounded so confused on the phone, I knew I had to do something. If you hadn't hung up on me, you would have heard me tell you that I needed a break. The legislature's out of session, and the Capitol's too quiet. Damn, Tyler. You can't handle this city all by yourself."

"I've been doing very well, thank you."

"Losing your girlfriend and picking up strange women. You call that good? I think it's Brooke, and I think it's got you all messed up."

"*Well.* I said *well.*"

"Well. Good. Whatever. I'm here."

"For how long?"

"Two weeks."

Two weeks was doable, and normally, Tyler enjoyed his brother's company. But he was already at the end of his rope between the hospital and Edie. Now he'd have to deal with Austen, too? And Brooke. Oh, yes, Austen would want to see Brooke. "I'm really busy. This endowment is important to me."

"Emma says that Max Lockwood is here." Austen looked at Tyler knowingly.

"Who?" asked Tyler, pretending ignorance.

"Max Lockwood," repeated Austen, and he then proceeded to rattle off every libelous name that Tyler had ever used in reference to Max, some alluding to poor medical skills, some questioning his sexual orientation and some referencing his mother's sexual relations with various members of the animal kingdom.

Tyler, who was not usually a squinter, squinted, mostly as a guise to feign confusion and befuddlement. Austen, who spent his life feigning confusion and befuddlement, was not fooled. "Is that what this is about? Some twenty-year-old grudge? That's why you're here in New York?"

"I'm furthering the advancement of medical science!"

Austen rubbed his eyes and then swore. "At least go out tonight. If not for me, think of the women. Do you really want to disappointment a lady, Tyler? I don't think so. You'd castrate yourself first."

"I can't."

"Why?"

"It's work," he lied.

"No it's not. Dr. Keating is flying to Boca. There is no 'work' scheduled."

"I can't."

"Why?"

"I have other plans."

"What sort of other plans? You don't make other plans?"

"I have plans."

Austen peered closer, his hat low over perceptive, beady eyes. "It's a female."

"She's a female," Tyler admitted.

"Who's the female?"

"No one."

"Some one is a female. Is this the 'odd phone call' female? Did you feel guilty for your harsh treatment of her and now you've got a pity date because you can't handle the pressure? If that's it, I can get you off the hook. Disappointing females is my reason for being on this planet."

It was at this point that Tyler knew his brother would not give up. Austen was too stubborn, and although Tyler would never admit it aloud, he knew Austen was worried about him. "It's a date. It's not a pity date, and I'm not breaking it."

"Cynthia?"

"No."

"Who?"

"Not Cynthia."

"Who?"

"Her name is Edie Higgins. You would like her." Austen would be all over drunken karaoke, he'd go bowling without an argument and he'd love to see Tyler sweat in embarrassment. Yes, Edie and Austen had much in common. At that, Tyler smiled. It was probably the reason he liked Edie so much.

"If I would like her, why are you taking her out?"

"I like her, too."

"Like, as in 'I like free beer,' or like, as in 'I like women to blow me,' like."

Tyler remained silent, and Austen leaned back against the seat and released a slow breath. "Holy…" And then: "I want to meet her."

"No."

"I want to meet her, or else I'm going to think she's some hospital groupie who's trying to get her hooks into you since you're heartbroken and on the rebound, and aren't thinking straight."

Austen grinned and Tyler knew that look. It was how Tyler ended up losing his virginity to Mrs. Porter at the age of fourteen. It was the reason he got suspended for smuggling a dissected pig into the high school cafeteria serving line. Tyler hated that look.

"Maybe," Tyler hedged.

Austen whistled. "Holy…"

"Stop."

"Okay. Let's go see Brooke," suggested Austen.

"No."

His brother slung an arm over the back of the couch. "I'm here. You're here. She's here. It's kismet."

"You flew on an airplane. I'm here for work. She lives here. There is no kismet."

"God, you're such buzz-kill. So what time's the hot date?"

"Eight."

"Well, come on then, time's a wasting. That's three hours of drinking that we get to do."

"I'm not getting drunk."

"Of course not," Austen said with a grin. "But first, we need to get you a cowboy hat."

AT EIGHT-THIRTY, EDIE had resigned herself to being stood up once again. Not that she'd been actually stood up for a date, she corrected. No, it was worse. She'd been stood up for a booty call.

She puttered around her apartment, stalling and making excuses, but the clock was incredibly loud, reminding her to leave. Maybe she'd go to the strip club. Anita was working. Jade was working. Men loved to see single women at a strip club. They would hit on her, they would soothe her ego and she could take out all her anger on Tyler, who apparently would not be present to see all that really pissed-off anger.

Just as she was sliding her feet into her shoes, the buzzer rang. Eight-forty-five? Not too bad, she told herself. And he was a surgeon, after all. Probably been out saving important lives. Maybe the Pope or something. In fact, Edie was so calm and collected that she even answered her door with a smile on her face. Yes, she could be perky and happy and cheerful.

Until she saw him. Slowly her smile dimmed.

There was Tyler. Snockered was the official term for it. His tie was charmingly loose. His hair was artfully mussed, and he leaned in her doorway, swaying only slightly.

Wearing a cowboy hat.

"Eeeedie," he said, as he stumbled in her general direction, wrapping his arms around her, and cupping her ass. "Glutumus. Maximumus. Lusciousus."

A cute and frisky drunk. She wanted to be furious at him, but he was so appealing, all that unbuttoned sincerity and partially upright virtue.

Snockered. In a cowboy hat.

"Tipsius much?" she asked, guiding him in the direction of her couch, watching as he took off the hat and tossed it Frisbee-style across the room where it hit a lamp.

The lamp would have to wait.

"It was never Austen's fault. Always mine," he explained, putting his head on her shoulder and his hand on her breast.

"Austen?"

"Bastard brother."

"He's here?"

"Not here."

"Then why is this Austen's fault?" she said, enunciating carefully, but she suspected it was too late because Tyler's eyes were starting to close.

"It was always Austen's fault," he muttered, his breathing starting to slow.

Carefully she eased away from him, but he held tight, curling into her, one hand firmly on her boob. Yes, Tyler Hart hid it well, but he was just as much a guy as the next dude.

But Edie didn't mind. In fact, she kind of liked him this way, all human and needy. No, she didn't mind at all, she thought as she pulled the throw from the back of her couch and settled them in for the night. She closed her eyes, listening to the quiet sounds of his breathing noting the quiet flutters in her heart.

The next morning, sunshine hit her eyes and she looked around for Tyler, but he had already gone, leaving only a note:

We didn't go to the museum, did we? Don't remember. I probably owe you an apology. I'm sorry if I did something I shouldn't have done, or didn't do something I should have done.

It's all Austen's fault. He's in NY. We'll go out to
dinner. Much fun.
Not.
Soberly yours,
Tyler.

AUSTEN HART WAS A FEW inches taller than his brother, a
few inches broader than his brother, and what Tyler lacked
in immediate charm and warmth, Austen made up for in
spades.

It would be a contrary woman who wanted the serious
brother. The one with the go-it-alone gaze, the one with
the flatline of a mouth, the one of few words, who lived
and breathed for his work.

Dumb contrary woman.

As the night wore on, Edie felt her gaze tracking back to
the serious one, and while Austen flirted with the waitress,
Edie pondered the folly of her own contrary heart.

Austen listened politely as Edie retold her repertoire of
"only in New York" stories. He laughed at the exact perfect
spots, but after the plates were removed, it was Tyler's hand
she sought. Tyler's scrupulous fingers she locked with her
own.

Yes, the human heart was a finicky thing that frankly
didn't care what was good for it.

Austen was quick with the yarns, too, but she noticed
a common thread in the brothers' adventures. Tyler was
always the one to take care of Austen, always protecting
him, always defending him. Sure, Tyler denied most of it,
but it was one of those silly, macho bluffs.

And she'd be a fool to miss the love in Austen's eyes.
Or Tyler's. These two brothers were a pair, with their slow
talk and their gentlemanly old-world view of everything.

They were just about to order dessert, when Tyler's pager

went off. He looked at Edie, and his mouth worked into an apologetic smile. It was a look she was getting accustomed to, but it didn't bother her so much. And as a bonus, she could interrogate Austen at length without Tyler around. The evening was rife with possibilities of digging around for whatever miniscule skeletons existed.

"You'll behave?" Tyler asked Austen.

"Don't I always?" his brother replied, and Tyler turned to Edie.

"I'm sorry."

"It's all right," she said, and she realized that she meant it. "I have co—"

He stopped her with a hard kiss, leaving her slightly dazed and confused. In fact, she was so dazed and confused that she whispered to him words that had never before passed her lips: "Come over later. I'll be waiting."

As soon as he left, her fingers crept to her mouth, Jane Eyre-style, until she caught herself and tucked them in the folds of her napkin.

Wretched moonstruck fingers.

Austen, the more emotionally astute brother, was watching with curious eyes. "Well, you're certainly not Cynthia. I don't think she ever wore a green streak in her hair. Now don't get me wrong, it's a good look for you. Edgy."

Edie put a hand to her head, pushing aside the streak. A defensive gesture—no, siree. "I'm the rebound affair. Hot sex with the flaky hippie chick. It's a wounded-pride thing," she added with an extra dose of flaky hippie chick in her voice.

"Far be it from me to interfere in my brother's private affairs, but actually, I interfere fairly regularly, and I gotta tell you, he's acting almost human."

"Has he always been like this?"

"You mean serious, dedicated, with an aversion to fun? Not always. Most of it was nurtured."

She waited for him to continue, but apparently he was done, sipping at his beer and grinning at Edie as if the whole thing was a joke. Edie wasn't fooled.

"Your father?"

Austen shrugged, an "I don't want to talk about it" gesture much like his brother's.

Unfortunately, Edie believed that everyone felt better after they talked. It was conversational therapy, nothing more. "What was it like?"

He laughed, and it almost sounded genuine, but Edie knew fake laughter, too. "More like what it wasn't like. Frank didn't hit us, but he didn't help us, either. He liked to sit in his chair, drink and ponder the many ways that life had kicked him in the ass. Eventually, I stopped listening. Not Tyler. He took it personally and molded it into his own quest for human perfection. Tyler figured if he was perfect, Frank would stop pointing out the flaws in us. But that's Tyler. Lots of times, he'd miss the most obvious things. As such, Ty graduated at the top of his class in medical school, and Frank still never stopped complaining."

Dr. Jordan Higgins had never been one to sit in his chair and complain. It was the first time that Edie registered a positive in locus absent parentus. And she had a really cool mom. Yes, a lonely, cool mom, but still... "Your mother wasn't around?" she asked.

"She was the smart one. She left when I was a baby. We're not sure about the rest."

Edie noticed the momentary frown, and that from a man who obviously wasn't a frowner. "And you don't want to know."

"He told you about Brooke?"

Brooke? Who was Brooke? "Oh, yeah," Edie assured him. "Not that he said a lot, you know, being Tyler," she hedged, because Edie knew that this was important. Family was important.

"He doesn't want to see her. I don't want to see her, but since we're both up here, and she's up here, it seems weird not to. You think that's weird?"

Edie, who understood the idiosyncrasies of the human condition better than most, shook her head. "Not weird. You have to be comfortable with your decisions."

Austen considered it. "Tyler thinks she's a con. We'd know if we had a sister."

Typical denial. Edie knew the signs. "Of course you would."

"But I think Tyler wonders about Mom and wants to know. He was only eight when she left, and you know that's going to leave some damage, but he's really stubborn about it. Did he say anything to you?"

"No, but like you said, he's not a big talker." She leaned her cheek on her palm, considering his placid face, the always-present smile. One good faker could always recognize another. "You should go see Brooke. Find out the truth. Better than hiding it and never knowing what might be."

"We're not hiding."

Edie quirked a brow. "No?"

"Not a lot," he answered, sounding exactly like his brother.

She shrugged, as if the whole thing was unimportant. "Maybe you're right—don't see her. Don't find out. Don't care, and spend the rest of your life wondering."

"I don't wonder," he protested.

She shot him a knowing look. "We all wonder. We all expect family to be some sort of ideal, but it's not. All families have their spots. Some have bigger spots than others, but in the end, the only ones you can count on, are the people you love."

"Maybe," he said, clearly unconvinced. Edie pulled out the big guns.

"Do it for Tyler. You know he wants to know about his mother. Settle it once and for all. He's hurting inside."

Edie didn't want him to hurt. She whined, complained, and groused to anyone who would listen, but when Tyler hurt, he never said a word at all.

Austen shrugged. "You're sure you're just the rebound affair?"

No, and that was the problem.

IT WAS TWO HOURS LATER, as Edie was lounging in her pink polka-dot baby-doll nightie, not waiting for Tyler, but yes, she was waiting for Tyler, when the esteemed Dr. Jordan Higgins phoned. At first, she was confused. Frankly, she wasn't sure he even knew her cell number, which yes, was overly critical, but Edie preferred being objective about her father.

"I didn't know you had this number."

"I got it from your mother," he answered.

Edie smiled, knowing that sometimes overly critical was exactly correct.

"Why didn't you tell me?" he asked.

"Tell you what?"

"Tyler. You're dating Dr. Hart."

There was approval in her father's voice. Pleasure. In slow motion, her universe twisted in upon itself and imploded.

"We're not dating, Daddy," she insisted, because she wasn't ready for this conversation.

"He said you were seeing each other, punkin."

When she saw Tyler, *if* she ever saw Tyler, she was going to correct his assumptions—after the sex, of course. No fool, here. "It's a physical thing, Daddy. More sex than anything."

"I don't want to hear this."

Satisfied, she continued, "He wants the endowment.

Bad. That is his prime directive at the moment, not a relationship with a waitress."

"A restauranteur," her father corrected.

Edie heard something strangely wonderful in his voice. Pride? Yes, that's what it was. She smiled in spite of everything. "He told you that? You two must've talked for a long time."

"Over a triple bypass."

In surgery? Doctors gossiped while in surgery? A picture popped into her head. Tyler in scrubs. Suturing. Clamping. "He's a good surgeon?"

"You should have seen him, Edie. Reminded me of my younger days. Sure, he was a little stubborn, a little too quick to dismiss any other ideas, but he sliced through that sternum like Julia Child carved chickens."

Edie didn't want to laugh, didn't want to approve, didn't want to feel the hero-worship vibes, but she did. "I'm glad you're glad. But don't get crazy. This is temporary."

"He's coming to the gala. Said you were coming, too."

Edie frowned. "He did?"

"Sure. I told your mother. She wanted to have drinks before. I told her it sounded like a great idea. You get yourself all dolled up, keep your hair one color, cover up the tattoo and put a doc on your arm. It's a first step, Edie. A big one. I knew you had it in you. You're a Higgins. Make me proud."

Her smile dwindled, the words sucking all the oxygen out of what had turned into a great conversation. After she hung up, Edie sat and watched an old movie, ignoring the clock, ignoring the new polish on her toes. What had been fun and exciting, now felt stifling.

Edie dug through her closet, pulling out the long black dress she'd worn to her cousin's wedding. It was elegant, classic, and when she tried it on, huge brown eyes stared back at her.

Mom would want her in diamonds, or pearls. The plunging neckline revealed the rose-colored edge to her tattoo.

It was Edie, but it wasn't Edie.

Her heart hammered double-time, and she stripped off the dress and threw on a short, royal blue skirt, yellow tank with chunky beads and bright yellow slides on her feet.

There, she thought to herself, and the girl in the mirror smiled back.

THERE WAS A MESSAGE on his phone.

"Meet me at the hotel."

Tyler wasn't sure what this was about, but he found her waiting for him just inside the lobby, leaning against a carved wooden post. When the men walked by her, he could see the heat in their eyes.

It wasn't the way she was dressed, it was the daring in her eyes, the confident smile on her lips. Tonight she was fire, a man touched her to burn.

Tyler approached, but didn't touch. He didn't need to. Heat was coming off her in waves.

"Let's go in," she said, nodding toward the viewing rooms. A couple walked past them, respectable, upstanding, ready to watch two strangers have sex.

"No."

"Scared?" she taunted, toying with him, playing with him. His cock happily grew.

"No."

"Have you ever watched anybody?"

"No." Then he corrected himself. "Once in high school. It was the homecoming game, and they were behind the bleachers and didn't think anyone could see them. I pretended I wasn't watching." Where had that come from? "You?" he asked casually.

"Watched anybody? Oh, yeah. All the time."

"Really?" Tyler asked, not quite ready to believe her.

Edie Higgins's mouth was a lot bigger than her life. Not that he minded because she had a cute mouth, especially when...

"My old roommate," she answered, interrupting his fantasy.

Really? "She had sex in front of you?"

"He. Barnaby. And it was only a few times."

"You lived with Barnaby? The cab driver?" He'd never liked the idea of Barnaby. Now he hated it with a dark passion, and he hadn't even met him.

"We didn't live together that way."

"There's only one way for a man to live with a woman."

"We didn't have sex, Tyler."

"But that doesn't mean he didn't want to."

"He only stayed with me until he found a place of his own."

"How long did that take?"

"Seven months. Come on," she told him.

When they entered the tiny room, Tyler swallowed, it felt like the edge of oblivion. He prayed that no one had been watching the first morning they'd been here, but then he noticed the seminaked couple on the bed, and Taylor opened his eyes a little wider.

Edie took his hand and they found themselves in a high-backed booth. In front of them were three four black walls, designed to muffle sound, and a glass wall, displaying the bedroom that Edie and Tyler had occupied before.

The theater.

EDIE'S FIRST INCLINATION was not to watch the couple on the bed, but the pair drew her eyes. The man had a shirt half-off, his pants undone. The woman's dress was down to her waist, up to her waist, and there were black shiny shoes on her feet. Edie told herself to focus on the shoes but the huge red bed with the rumpled covers snagged her attention.

She and Tyler...

Had...

There...

She wanted to stay blasé, sophisticated and unmoved, but if at that moment, Tyler chose to explore the depths of her panties, he would discover how completely moved she currently was.

His hand slipped up her bare thigh...and then it slipped higher. She kept her eyes glued to the glass case, her heart about to explode, waiting for the second when his fingers would touch here...

There...

Her body quivered at the torturous contact, her muscles clenching, and his finger began to play her with rich, languid strokes.

This time, she moaned.

The steady movements were so small, so precise, but...

Hell.

If she were as sophisticated, unmoved as she wanted to be, her thighs would fall open a little wider.

Like so.

Another clever finger slid across her lips, stroking her like a cat, and she curled upward because he felt so good.

The sounds of the other couple filtered through the speakers, low moans, quiet sighs, and when Edie slid lower in her seat, a quiet sigh escaped from her lips. Everything was so dark, so private, and she closed her eyes, wanting to bask in the fires of sex.

Cool air hit her thighs, and she realized that her favorite black thong was probably now on the floor. She shifted to meet Tyler's intense gaze, and the rest of the world slipped away. She wanted this. Him.

Now.

Purposefully, she climbed into his lap, her fingers at his fly, feeling the thick sex waiting for her.

Tyler didn't press her, didn't hurry her, merely watched her with those steady dark eyes. She freed his cock, slid her hands over the thick length and watched the drop of sweat beading on his forehead.

Not so unmoved, either.

Feeling more confident, Edie climbed fully into his lap and slipped her shirt over her head, baring her breasts. Another drop of sweat beaded at the sweet spot above his mouth. Delighted, she licked it away, and this time he groaned.

Her smile lasted a second before his mouth covered hers, devoured hers, and she could feel him between her thighs. Needing more, she moved one tiny inch, sighing into his mouth as he filled her.

This.

Sex wasn't supposed to be like floating in the ocean. Sex was supposed to be dangerous, mysterious. A single inconsequential moment in time. A transient experience of two bodies filling a need.

But when he held her, when he kissed her, when he filled her, it was so heady, so warm, so tempting to lose herself in him.

Her hands pushed aside his neat white shirt and found warm skin, beating heart, and she wrapped her arms around the broad planes of his back, holding him there, fusing two bodies into one.

Hungrily his mouth grazed her neck, the stubble at his jaw abrading her skin, and she could hear the steady sounds of his breathing against her ear. His cock filled her, then relinquished her, because that was the way of sex.

Stay. Go. *Stay.*

She didn't want to anticipate those moments when he was with her, inside her, but her body did. It expected it. Craved it. Needed it. Even while her body was happily satisfying itself, her mind rebelled. There was no drama, no flash, only one man, one woman, and when his hand nudged her head into his shoulder, Edie reluctantly pressed her check again the warm, damp skin and let her body ride.

How long she stayed there, Edie didn't know, but eventually her mind weakened and acquiesced. This pleasure was not the storm she wanted, but an easy current carrying her further out to sea. Tyler never wavered, the strong flex of his hips neither too fast nor too slow, filling her, releasing her as if there was all the time in the world.

In. Out. In. Out.

In.

Out.

In. In. In.

Her mouth sought his, locking her lips to his, and her tongue slipped inside, coyly playing, teasing, in and out, but his mouth trapped her, keeping her there, as if this was no game.

Reminding herself that this was a game, Edie lifted her body from his, relinquishing him, the lips of her sex brushing against his cock, teasing him, playing. Impatiently, she waited for his reaction, frustration, laughter, anger... anything but this. Tyler met her eyes, steady, constant, and she nearly screamed at him, anything to rock the boat, anything to lift the tide.

"Edie," he whispered, devil-soft, and she knew what that word meant. It was an invitation. A temptation. A joining. Be. With. Me.

All around her, women responded to those words, were lured by the idea of them, and Edie had always judged them for their gullibility. For their weakness. The speakers in the room amplified the noise of others having sex, and Edie clung to those sounds, but the temptation in his eyes was louder, stronger, and eventually her eyes drifted closed, her sex closed over his cock as if it belonged and her cheek pressed against his shoulders, leaning, resting.

Weak.

13

ON TUESDAY, TYLER HAD three surgeries, two consults, one presentation, drinks with his brother, and then a night with Edie.

Every time he thought they were fine, he would say something, suggest something, and he could see the walls rise. But they had time, he had time, all he had to do was not screw it up.

Or screw up anything else.

The surgeries went well, he noticed Keating nodding in agreement during the presentation, and he had made tomorrow's reservations for Edie's surprise. Another step, and hopefully she wouldn't be mad. Tyler could've asked for his brother's advice but taking relationship advice from Austen was like taking medical advice from Dr. Death. Besides, for the past few days, Austen had been on at him to visit Brooke.

Their sister.

And now, Edie and Austen had joined forces. Both with their guilelessly innocent looks, as if he didn't know what they were thinking. Unfortunately, Austen was getting to him, Edie was getting to him.

He could feel insidious doubts snaking through his cerebral cortex like a caduceus gone wrong.

Get it over with. Just do it.

He was being tag-teamed by Machiavellian manipulators and even knowing that, he wondered if he were wrong.

Wrong?

He was still purging that impossible thought from his head when he met Austen at a sports bar, where his brother was chatting up the waitress and betting against the Yankees.

Tyler joined him at the bar. "You know that's a hanging offense up here."

Austen took a long swallow of whiskey and sighed with deep appreciation. "Life's too short to not stir the shit. So how much time am I slotted tonight?"

Tyler liked the sarcasm because words, even sarcastic ones were better than awkward silences. Edie told him families were often sarcastic, that it was a sign of affection. The way he saw it, sarcasm was good. "We've got ninety minutes. I don't want to be late again. I'm trying to prove to her that all surgeons aren't overworked automatons with no understanding of balanced, mutually supportive, male-female courtship rituals."

"Good luck with that," Austen said with a snicker. His gaze flickered back to the game, but it was an act. Austen knew how to set up his prey. "Why are you doing this? For her, or some never-ending quest to better yourself?"

"Both," Tyler replied, and then corrected his answer because he liked the sound of the truth. "Her."

Austen had never cared about success or approval. He was always comfortable in his own skin, but not Tyler. Tyler's skin always felt one size too small, one stone too heavy.

Until Edie.

She never looked at him as if he needed to be more or do more. She made him reckless...and happy. He didn't want to forget that happy part. It was important.

"Good for you, Ty. Carpe diem. Hakuna matuta, and all that other foreign stuff that tells people to have a good time because it isn't a part of the American work ethic. Sucks."

Tyler clinked his glass to Austen and they sat there in silence. Austen watched the baseball game, and Tyler studied the trading cards under the glass bar. He'd never played baseball, never did sports. If they had had somebody in the house other than Frank, maybe...

But they didn't.

"I shouldn't want to see Brooke."

Austen turned and looked at him. "What if we take the train up to meet her, and everything turns out okay?"

"Because it doesn't. You never rely on chance. You take charge of your decisions and when you're ahead, you walk away. We're ahead now, Austen. I turned out great, and you aren't in prison. Life's good. I should leave well enough alone."

"Maybe it could be better. You've always wanted to be up here. You're up here. Edie's a total babe, ten times better than anyone you've ever been with before. You're whipping Lockwood's ass? Right?"

When Austen framed it like that, it did sound almost positive. "Maybe."

"Go for it, Tyler. Take a shot. Take a chance. Throw the dice and see how the other half of our family actually lived. I've got a good feeling about this."

"The last time you had a good feeling, you burned down the shed."

"It wasn't so bad, even then."

Tyler shook his head. "You're going to make me do this?"

"Dude, nobody makes you do anything you don't want to do. The fact that we're even having this conversation means you know I'm right."

"Maybe," Tyler said, but then quickly changed the subject. "What are you looking for, Austen?"

"Nothing but net. A cushy job, good whiskey and a life of perpetual sex."

"Don't you ever want to be with someone?"

"It's all about the journey, Tyler. It's no fun without the games. Go find Edie. Get laid, bro. It'll do you good."

Tyler paid for the drinks and left the bar to go do just that, and for the moment, his sister was forgotten.

DÉJÀ VU WAS TERMED "tedious familiarity" in the dictionary. Tedious, implying tiresome, or in the colloquial sense, total pain in the ass. As such, when Edie sat alone in her apartment, watching the clock tick, the term *déjà vu* singsonged in her head with tedious familiarity. At nine o'clock the text message came:

Keating wants me in surgery. Sorry. Will pick you up tomorrow at 2.

Calmly, Edie changed from the black silk teddy into something more appropriate for the diner, grabbed the work schedules for the next month and headed for her home away from home.

Work.

At the diner, Patience and Anita were on the floor, Stella was on the grill and Khandi was watching CNN in the back.

"Edie," Anita called out to her.

"Got next month's schedule," Edie announced, pushing open the kitchen door and posting it on the crowded bulletin board, directly under the health notice, a defaced ad for a dating service and the data for next month's book club.

"You have me working on Father's Day?"

"No," Edie told her, because she had covered all the requests, and wouldn't have missed one from Anita.

"Be a doll and cover for me, will you? Big night at the club."

"Father's Day? Really?"

"Oh, yeah. Tips are awesome. You can cover, can't you?"

Edie's first instinct was to say yes because Anita needed her help, and when people needed her help, Edie always said yes, even when some times she experienced regrets later, which took some of the joy out of the "doing good" experience. However, she was also realizing that she didn't want to necessarily spend all her free time covering shifts so that others could live their lives.

She had a life, she thought to herself. She had use for free time. She had limited free time. Her limited free time was becoming more valuable now, and as such, she needed to protect the resource. "Why don't you switch with Wanda? She likes to work Sunday nights?"

Anita stared at her oddly, but then said, "Sure."

As the hours passed by, Edie redid the menus, helped Wanda study for her history exam, debated with her mother about the wisdom of buying a Father's Day gift for the man who has everything and dodged questions about one currently absent Dr. Tyler Hart.

Finally, the sun came up, Ira dragged himself in for the morning shift, the food deliveries were all put away. When she arrived back at her place, Edie set the alarm for 1:00 p.m. and crawled into bed.

Alone.

Screw déjà vu.

IT WAS A REALLY GOOD THING that the weather was gorgeous, that Riverside Park was quiet, that the roses were blooming, because after last night, Edie was both tired and undersexed. She was a woman on the edge....

Until she saw the bike.

"I promised," Tyler told her proudly and she remembered that he did.

It was a tandem. Shiny blue with two seats, two wheels and two sets of pedals. When she spoke, her voice was soft, sounding not so tired, and more than a little goofy. "I distinctly remember saying the words *a momentary joining of two bodies*...this bicycle is not sexual. It implies a visual social connection and easy conversations."

"You did promise to teach me."

She narrowed her eyes. "The student has surpassed the master. At this point, we're all about the sex. This is not sex."

Tyler looked completely unfazed. "People can have sex on bicycles."

She pointed to the two seats. "Here?"

He scratched his head. "Probably not, but I'll cop a feel if it'll make you think more of me."

Her instincts told her to scoff at the togetherness such a vehicle implied, but he was waiting, watching her steadily, and the day was glorious and the ice cream trucks were out and Dr. Tyler Hart was nervous.

It was enough to make someone melt. It was more than enough to make Edie smile and press a kiss to his mouth. "I love it."

"I knew that," he said, and climbed on the front. "You're in back. Sorry. Get used to the balance, the feel of the pedals, the dizzying height from the ground."

"Are you mocking me?" she asked, taking the backseat, wishing he were a little closer.

"Doctors do not mock. They only assess the situation

and when some chickenshit looks at the terra firma with anxiety in her eyes..."

She tried to whack at him, but he was just out of her reach. So close, so far. So irresistible.

She tried to be a hard-ass, but she failed. His was a nervy smile, and she shot him a nervy smile in return. At that, his expression grew cocky, and she knew that he knew that he had her.

Damn it.

They rode up the sidewalk, down the pier, past joggers and other serious, more obnoxiously adept bicyclists, but Edie didn't care. Tyler was not making fun of her nerves, the ground wasn't as far as she thought, and so far, her balance was perfect.

Besides, directly in front of her was a studly young man, decked out in T-shirt and shorts.

As they rode, he pointed out various technical aspects of the bike, and she admired the broad lines of his back, the way his efficient legs pumped up and down as if they could ride forever. When he turned around, perhaps he noticed the lust in her eyes.

"Where to now?"

"My apartment is four blocks from here," she suggested.

Surprisingly perceptive—maybe not that surprisingly— he wheeled them around and she ogled those long efficient legs until they were back in her apartment, and she had him naked and on top of her.

She stared into those dark, steady eyes, and Edie tightened her hold even tighter, using efficient legs as if she could ride him forever.

In her heart, she thought she could.

14

THE NEXT MORNING, EDIE awoke with Tyler next to her, watching her with serious eyes. "Will you come with me?"

"Where?" she asked, even though she knew.

"Cold Springs. To see my sister."

"I thought you didn't want to go." There was a resigned weariness in his face, and although she understood it, she wished she had the power to take it away.

"I don't. I think it's a mistake and mistakes can't be undone."

"Then why go?"

"Austen thinks it's a good idea, and for the past twelve months, it's metastasized inside him, so I know he's going to go up there and talk to her and find out all the miserable things that he'd be better off not knowing. When he does that, I'd rather I was there. He told me he wanted me there." Tyler smiled at that, as if something miraculous had happened. Edie thought it had.

"So why do you want me to go?" she asked, wondering if there was space in the world for two miracles in one day.

"Because when I hear all the miserable things that I'd be better off not knowing, I'd rather you were there."

Gently she kissed him, touched more than words.

This is what people did.

They needed each other.

Edie knew she needed Tyler, and now her heart knew that he needed her, too.

BROOKE WASN'T ANYTHING like what he'd expected her to be. She was short, petite, with long, dark hair. There were no streaks in it like Edie's. No, Brooke Campbell had neat, normal hair. While Tyler sat in the middle of his sister's living room, he found himself wishing badly for a page from the hospital, an onslaught of a new pandemic, or a nuclear explosion.

"I'm glad you came. I know this has been difficult," his sister was saying.

"Not at all," Tyler replied with a flat smile. Edie grabbed hold of his hand as if he needed her assistance. Not wanting to disappoint her, he held it tightly as if he didn't want to let go.

"This is a great place," gushed Austen, who was currently roaming the room, taking in the old photos of their mother, her second husband, their baby. There were pictures of the Grand Canyon, the Eiffel Tower, the U.S. Capitol. It was storybook, the Great American Family. Tyler felt something curdle in his stomach. Maybe it was food poisoning? Maybe he could swallow hemlock?

As if sensing his thoughts, Edie gave him a smile and he managed a half smile in return.

"I wanted to talk to you before the hospital gala."

Tyler raised his head. "What was that?"

"My fiancé. He's a sales rep for Lifeline Pharmaceuticals. I thought you would like that. That you two have something in common. Medicine."

Tyler wasn't sure what he was supposed to say. When in doubt keep your mouth shut. He didn't have to wait long because apparently Brooke didn't like the silence. "Mother was really cool. You would have liked her."

"I don't remember much about her," Austen said. No, Austen wouldn't remember much about her. Not even the day she left. He'd been playing baseball. Frank had been at work. Only Tyler had been home when she left.

Yes, he remembered her well.

"She did a lot of work for the PTA. Reading in the classrooms, volunteering at the food pantry at the church. She taught me Latin when I was eight."

"What about your father?" asked Tyler. "What did he do?" Gas station attendant, porn king, mafioso?

"He was a church pastor. Most likely you drove by his church on your way here."

"He's dead now?" asked Tyler, and Edie pressed her nails into his hand.

Brooke looked down at her lap, the picture of the bereaved daughter.

"Yes. He passed away three years before Mother did. I don't think she ever recovered after he died. They really loved each other."

Tyler was going to throw up. By this time, even Austen was starting to look a little green. It wasn't the family failure that Tyler had envisioned, instead, in many ways, this was worse.

"I found Austen's birth certificate in Mother's safety deposit box and I looked you up on the internet."

Goddamned Google.

"I've always wanted a real family and when I found out about… At first, I wasn't sure what to say, so thus the hang-up calls. Sorry. But how to tell someone, 'Hey, your mother died, and, oh, by the way, I'm your sister.'"

You don't.

Edie, tenderhearted Edie, smiled nicely at Brooke. "It must have been hard."

"Not as hard as it must have been for you two," she said, nodding to Austen and Tyler, her face drawn into some Mother Teresa portrait of sympathy.

Tyler rose. "Actually, it's been easy. And this has been great. I think I'm going to leave now."

Edie shot him a nervous glance. "You're sure?"

"I'm due in surgery."

Austen picked up his hat, dusted it off, as if there were dirt on the brim and met Tyler's eyes for one long, moment. In his little brother's face, he saw the one thing he'd wanted to avoid at all costs. The hard realization that life could be shit.

EDIE TOOK ONE HASTY GLANCE toward the door, and then noticed the disappointment in Brooke's expression. "I'm sorry," she told her.

"It's all right. I expected too much. I'm about to get married—"

"Congratulations."

"I want everything to be perfect. My parents, they were so in love, so perfect, and I thought everything *was* perfect until I realized what she'd done. Still, I was excited to know I had two brothers."

"They weren't quite so excited as you," Edie pointed out, because Brooke should be aware that not everyone had a fairy-tale life, and now that she was experiencing it first-hand—the perfectly turned out living room, the lifeless pictures on the wall—Edie decided that a fairy-tale life wasn't all it was cracked up to be.

"I had hoped we could be friends. Do all the family things. Thanksgiving dinners, taking portraits..." Her eyes were wistful. Odd.

"Why'd she leave them?"

"I don't know. There were a lot of things about her that I never understood, but she always tried to be a great mom."

"It sounds like she was." Edie noted the picture on the mantel. Tyler's mother stood in front of a church, with glorious spring flowers and a spiffy Easter hat. It was like something out of a magazine, except for the woman's hard eyes and haggard face. Edie's smile was tight, because frankly, she had decided that Charlene Hart was a world-class monster for leaving her two sons behind, but obviously, Brooke wouldn't want to hear that.

"I should go." Edie headed for the door. Tyler was waiting. Austen was waiting, and Edie would be damned if she'd disappoint them. No, Brooke Campbell was a nice person, but Edie's loyalties were with Tyler. Always and forever.

"Yes. Thank you for coming. I'll see you next month at the gala."

"Oh, yes. Looking forward to it," Edie told her politely.

It was going to be hell.

AUSTEN TOOK A CAB BACK to his hotel, and Edie went with Tyler to the Belvedere. Once inside, he stood near the window, silent and still. But he was neither underneath. Edie could tell.

She wrapped her arms around him, and leaned her head against his back, resting there, feeling the pain that was radiating from him. She didn't understand how someone could walk away from Tyler. Not as a boy, not as a man. "I'm sorry."

"Don't be. It's done. Now maybe she'll leave us alone."

"Will you be all right at the gala? We don't have to go."

There was a desperation in him, a pain, and she didn't

protest. For once, Edie would be the strong one, and let him draw from her.

Draw from her he did, over and over. Her back was wet with sweat, and she could hear the labored rasp of his breathing, the buzz of the traffic below them until finally his movements began to slow, then still.

His hands wrapped around her once again, gently this time, and she could feel his face against her back, buried there, drawing comfort. "I'm sorry," he whispered, pressing a kiss to her skin.

She turned and held his face in her hands and pressed a kiss to his jaw, his cheek, the corner of his mouth, and then he took over the kiss with passion and desperation. She felt the frenzied beat of his heart against hers. He carried her to the bed, and made love to her again, making sure she found her pleasure, and later they lay together, two bodies entwined. Quietly Edie stroked his hair, until finally at peace, Tyler slept.

15

TYLER WENT WITH HIS BROTHER to the airport the next day. He didn't like the hard expression on Austen's face. Austen was the idealist, the dreamer, the kid most likely to work for the space program because his head was always in the clouds. But seeing the tic in his jaw was hard to take. It said that Tyler hadn't looked out for his brother the way he knew he should have. Once again. "This was a bad idea."

Austen shot him a tight-lipped smile. "You always have the exact perfect thing to say, Ty."

"Sorry."

Austen shrugged, shifting his bag over his shoulder. "Hey, no big deal. We move on. Life's too short to dwell on the fact that our family life sucked, our mother well and truly deserted us, and never mentioned once that she had two sons to our sister. No. It's all peachy."

"I'll fly down to Texas after the fellowship is over. We'll hit Sixth Street." He flicked the brim of Austen's hat. "I'll bring mine."

"I don't need a babysitter."

"Yeah, I remember the last time you said that. The shed burned down."

"Good times," Austen said, and then checked his watch. "Stick with Edie, Tyler. You need her."

Not sure what to say, Tyler only nodded, and watched his baby brother leave. Slowly he climbed into a taxi, remembering the first night he met Edie. Remembering everything. Need was a dangerous thing, always a harbinger of pain.

As the taxi pulled in front of Edie's building, he remembered the old joke. The doctor asks, "Does it hurt when you do this?" The punchline was the killer.

Then don't do it.

JUNE PASSED IN A RUSH. Edie spent a lot of her nights at the diner because she didn't want to stay home alone. Tyler worked long hours, and sometimes he would crawl into her bed, curling up next to her and falling asleep. She told herself to stay detached, but it wasn't much help.

He wouldn't talk about his cases, and sometimes she wanted to ask, but she didn't. Theirs was a cautious relationship, both treading lightly, not quite knowing where to step, where not to.

Her mother was pleased about the gala, and Edie had gone shopping. Bought a new dress. A beautiful maroon gown with simple lines. It wouldn't cover her tattoo, but at least she was coordinated, and for the night of the gala, hopefully everyone would be pleased.

Her father, and especially Tyler.

It was becoming more and more important to her, making Tyler happy.

THE BALLROOM OF THE Peninsula Hotel was decorated in silvery ribbons and pale gold balloons, and accented with tiny twinkling lights. Tyler had never been much for parties. He was never comfortable with meaningless chatter and worn-out jokes.

Across the room, Dr. Keating was talking to Lockwood and Edie's father. Tyler told his feet to walk across the room and join them, told them to walk across the room and make up some stupid joke.

Tyler's feet refused.

Smart feet.

Underneath the Lifeline Pharmaceuticals banner, Brooke was there with a man who was apparently her fiancé. He looked nice enough. Quickly, Tyler went back to the table where Edie was waiting for him. No, his feet didn't have any problem with that decision.

Smart feet.

Edie slipped her arm through his. "You know, if you keep grimacing like that, your face will freeze."

He worked up to a deathly grin.

She shook her head. "No. Stick to the grimace. It looks more honest."

At exactly half past nine, Dr. Abe Keating announced to all that this year's winner of the ACT/Keating Endowment Award was Dr. Max Lockwood.

Politely Tyler clapped.

Edie sat next to him, whispered in his ear, "Just wait 'til the patients start dropping like flies. Then they'll rethink that stinkin' award."

The words were meant to cheer him up, an off-the-cuff joke to make him feel more superior, more capable, because Tyler's patients never died.

Yeah, right.

While Dr. Keating was expounding on this year's accomplishments, Tyler excused himself and called the hospital.

"Any change?"

"She's still in ICU."

"Right," answered Tyler and went back to the ballroom where Edie was waiting for him, talking to an elegant woman who shared more than a passing resemblance to Edie—if one overlooked the pink streak in Edie's hair. Not that it mattered.

Tyler, say hello to Edie's mother. Tell her that you're delighted to be here. That you love New York. That Edie has been a great help to you.

His feet moved toward the group and he managed a smile.

"Mom. Dr. Tyler Hart. Tyler, Clarice Higgins, holy sainted mother, venerated above all in her eternal patience."

Mrs. Higgins shushed her daughter, and extended her hand.

"Hello," mustered Tyler, "You look very lovely tonight," he said truthfully, and Edie's mother blushed with pleasure.

"Thank you for that," she said, while Edie looked on with approval.

"I've taught him everything he knows."

He looked at his sister, and then looked away.

Edie noticed. "You need a drink?"

"No."

"You're going to stand here and be a lump."

"Yes."

"I need a drink. Let's get something and go out on the patio."

In a few seconds, they were outside, the trees covered in glimmering lights, too. The moon shone down and when Edie looked up at him, Tyler caught his breath.

Edie touched his arm, and he stared into warm brown eyes, caring eyes, loving eyes, and he pulled her close. "You look very nice, as well."

"Nice?"

"Hot?"

"Better."

"You look lovely. I wish I had the words to tell you, Edie. I wish I was better at talking, at emoting, at expressing, at communicating, but..."

"That's a good start."

Tyler kissed her, pressed her back against a tree, his hips grinding against her, wishing they were someplace else. Someplace alone. Someplace far away from the world.

"That's a better start," she told him, smiling tenderly.

He pulled back, and stared at her, mesmerized by the careless beauty of her. Sometimes the magic was too perfect, sometimes the world spun his way, sometimes, sometimes... Deciding to risk it all, he unlocked his heart. Just once. Only once. "I love you."

There was a second when he could almost hear her words. The mind did that some times. Filled in pieces of what it *thought* should have happened, instead of what had really happened. But Edie was always quick on her feet, she pressed her mouth to his, her tongue playing between his lips, seducing him, distracting him.

Almost loving him. But not quite.

Not nearly enough.

AFTER DINNER, TYLER WATCHED his sister and her fiancé. His name was Peter. "Call him Pete" was what he told everyone who would listen. Brooke was more interested in watching the party than watching Peter, but Tyler told himself it was none of his business.

Who the hell cared what happened in his sister's life?

He got a shot of whiskey from the bartender and wandered back onto the patio, wanting to see if Edie would follow him. A test.

He heard a sound behind him and turned, smiling, but it wasn't Edie, it was Brooke.

"Hello," she said. "It's a lovely party."

"Yeah, right."

"I didn't want this to be awkward. I was hoping you'd like me but it's as if I've done something wrong and I'm not sure what."

"Why don't you go back to Pete, Brooke?"

"I'm sorry," she said, and then turned to go, but before she could leave, he needed to say one last thing.

"If you don't love him, why don't you tell him?"

Slowly she turned. "What?"

"You don't love him. You're using him. Tell him. Don't let him get hurt."

She stared at Tyler, her eyes wide with shock. "He's my fiancé. I do love him."

"Enough?"

"Enough for what?"

"Enough for more than the parties? Enough for the not-so-awesome parts?" Once he started, the words wouldn't stop, and Brooke was staring at him as if he'd lost his mind.

He had.

He'd lost his mind. He'd lost his heart, and he was taking it out on a stranger.

Finally admitting that this wasn't a battle she could ever win, his sister fled.

Smart feet.

Must be something in the genes.

THE SHADOWS LIT ALONG her bedroom wall, adding an extra gloom to the night. Outside the window, life went on. Inside, the quiet was starting to kill her.

Tyler shifted, so careful not to touch her, and she hated that he couldn't touch her, hated that this was her fault. He loved her. It should be a cause for celebration, but instead, all she could hear in her head was...

Why can't you be something else? Something other than a doctor. Something not quite so perfect.

She longed to put her head on his chest, curl up close to him, and keep the doubts at bay. Always the doubts. Edie had known the doubts existed, but they'd never been so thunderously loud, so ear-splitting. So terrifying.

They stayed that way until Tyler rose, and began pulling on his clothes.

"I don't want to do this. If someone is going to leave in this relationship, I'd prefer that I was the one."

Even as she watched him dress, she tried to tell herself that it was the expected parting from a meaningless affair, but the pit in her stomach said otherwise. Stupid stomach. "Why do you need to leave?"

"I didn't get the endowment, Edie. The fellowship is over. I'm going back to Houston."

Unless you stay.

"Why are we here?" he asked.

She knew he was waiting for her. Waiting for her to break down and confess her feelings, waiting for her to promise undying love. Waiting for her to promise to wait for him every night while he basked in glory, and she wallowed in pearls. "We have a connection, a momentary joining of two bodies moving toward some feeling of soulful humanity."

"No, Edie. That's crap. It's there in your face, but you keep spouting the same things over and over again. I'm done."

"Don't go," she told him quietly.

"Why? You're going to spread your legs, blow me, set up a threesome? Is that what you think is keeping me here?"

There was a time when she would have laughed at that, thrown out some suggestive innuendo, but not now, not here, not with Tyler, of the oh-so-steady-and-lovely eyes. Not while he was leaving her.

"Get out."

"Happy trails, Edie. Go find yourself some bohemian poet who isn't a threat to your nice, safe view."

After he left, Edie lay in bed, telling herself that it was better this way, but the for the first time, Edie recognized her own lies for what they were.

16

FOR THE NEXT THREE DAYS, Edie lived at the diner, staying far away from Tyler's hotel, staying far away from his life. She told herself it was an impossible situation, that they were too different, that she knew what she wanted in life, and being a surgeon's wife wasn't it.

Unfortunately, there was a tiny voice inside her that knew what she did want.

Dr. Tyler Hart.

After the lunch rush was done, she saw a familiar face at table seventeen.

Her father.

He was there in his suit, his tie perfectly knotted, and for once, her father was waiting for *her*.

"This is a surprise," she started, sliding into the seat across from him. "Mom's birthday coming up? Want to know what to get her?"

Panic flashed in his eyes and she laughed. "Sorry, Dad. Habits. Mom's birthday is in the fall."

"I knew that," he told her, but then his face grew serious. "I was sorry to hear about the endowment, but Lockwood's a good surgeon."

"Not as good as Tyler," Edie answered, needing to defend him.

"No. Not as good as Hart. He's got a quick mind and a great set of hands, but he's never going to be a superstar. Do you know why?"

"No."

"He's got a weak heart. He cares too much. The fatal flaw."

"Why is that a flaw?"

"Because he lets his cases get to him. He can't walk away, and he's got to be able to walk away."

Edie studied her father's face, and realized that there was something more to this story. "What happened on Friday?"

"A patient died."

"Who?"

"I don't know." Her father peered at her closely. "You should ask him."

"Maybe." She wasn't ready to make promises. Not yet.

"'Maybe' doesn't cut it in life, Edie. Sometimes it's a split second, and you need to decide, and the maybes only end up with somebody dead."

"And a surgeon would think that way, wouldn't he?"

"Only way to be," he stated. "So who is Ira?" he asked, looking at the grizzled old man on the front cover of the menu.

"He's a cook."

"And you named the diner after him?"

"I thought it sounded like a diner-owner name."

"I think Edie sounds like a diner-owner name. I'm very fond of that name."

"Maybe, Dad. Maybe."

"No, no maybes, Edie."

"I'll do it," she agreed. Then she leaned over and kissed

him on the cheek. "You're not as bad as I thought. Not as great as everybody else thinks, though."

He held a finger to his lips. "That's our secret. Whatever you do, don't tell your mom."

THAT AFTERNOON, EDIE found herself at St. Agnes hospital. No, she corrected herself. She *decided* to be at St. Agnes hospital. To talk to Tyler. To fix things before he walked out of her life forever.

Edie told herself she was good at fixing things, she prided herself on fixing things. Hopefully, she would be as talented at fixing herself.

The lobby was crowded with people. Nurses, doctors, staff, patients, friends and family members. She pressed the elevator button to go upstairs when she noticed the older man next to her looking at her closely.

"You're with Dr. Hart?"

For a moment she was confused, but then she recognized the guard from the Empire State Building. The one who had let them upstairs.

"You know Dr. Hart?"

"He was my wife's doctor," he told her and then she could see the bobbing lump in his throat. "She passed Friday last."

Friday last? The night of the gala. All the pieces clicked into place, and Edie felt like a first-class jerk. "I'm very sorry," she said, reaching out for his hand.

"You'll tell Dr. Hart thank you," he said, blinking back the tears. Why did men always need to be so strong? Why did men always need to hide when they hurt?

"I'll tell him," she promised, and this time, Edie knew she would.

EDIE FOUND A COMFORTABLE couch in the waiting area and settled herself in. Hospitals had never been her favorite place. In fact, they were probably no one's favorite place. People came here when they were sick, in hopes of leaving healed, but not everyone could be healed.

Not Mrs. Heeney.

It took a strong person to work here, knowing that not everyone could be healed. Knowing that not every heart could be saved.

A strong person like Tyler.

A nurse appeared, holding a box of tissues. "Here. Can I get you some water? Are you waiting for someone?"

Edie wiped at her tears. "I don't need any water. I'm waiting for Dr. Hart."

"He may be in surgery for some time."

She managed a smile. "I can wait."

It was five hours until she saw him. He came out of surgery, pulled his cap off his head and then spotted her.

He came toward her with his doctor's face, eyes careful, mouth serious, but she knew his secrets. Edie knew what Dr. Tyler Hart tried to hide from the rest of the world.

Dr. Tyler Hart cared.

What sort of shifty coward *wouldn't* love a man like that? A great man who saved lives on a daily basis. Not Edie Higgins. Not anymore.

"I'm sorry," she apologized.

He stood still for a moment, before taking a seat in the chair opposite her. "For what?"

"For leaving."

"I was stupid. You didn't need to come here to say sorry to me." He pushed his hair out of his eyes, but she stopped him with her fingers, and stroked the silky strands away.

"I came here for you."

His gaze told her he was cautiously optimistic. Wasn't that what the medical professionals always said? Cautiously optimistic, as if they wanted to hope, but never could. It was all right because now Edie had enough optimism for both of them.

"I was wrong," she told him, needing to get that out there first.

"About what?"

"About us."

"It doesn't matter. I lost the endowment."

"I know. I'm sorry. You deserved it."

"No."

"I saw Mr. Heeney at the elevators. I'm sorry."

"It happens. It's part of the job."

"You could have told me. You could have told me that you hurt. I don't want you to hurt."

Tyler looked at her with steadfast eyes. "You get used to the Mrs. Heeneys of the world."

"Really? Sometimes don't you feel it here?" she asked, putting a hand to his chest.

He shrugged as if it didn't matter, as if he didn't care, but Edie wasn't giving up. Not anymore. From now on, she was in for the long haul—whatever it took.

"I love you," she told him, laying her heart on the line. "Please stay in New York, Tyler. You're carrying around my heart in there, too. I don't want to lose it. I don't want to lose you."

Because he was stubborn, he shook his head. "You won't be happy. You don't like to be alone."

Wisely she smiled, because now Edie understood. "I won't be. You're with me. You're always with me. When you're sitting next to me, when you're inside me, when you're two thousand miles away. You're here," she said, pointing to her own chest. "I'm never alone. Not anymore."

Something sparked in his eyes. Cautious optimism. Hope. "What about the patients? What if they come up and tell you how great I am?"

"You are great," she told him, grinning. "I might even agree."

But still, he wasn't convinced. "Someday I might have a building named after me. Probably a wing, not an entire building, but wouldn't it bug you?"

She shook her head. "No. I'm renaming the diner. Edie's. It's not a hospital wing, but it counts."

"Dr. Keating offered me an attending," he said.

Edie sighed in quick relief. "I know. Dad told me. You should take it."

"It's not the endowment—"

"But it counts." She locked her fingers around his because she wasn't about to let him go. Not now. Not ever. "Stay, Tyler. Please. Stay for me. Stay with me," she finished.

"I'll have to deal with Lockwood on a daily basis."

"I've heard sex goes a long way in soothing the savage beast," she countered.

And finally, he smiled. Once. A quick nervy smile. A smile that she loved. "As a trained medical professional, I can definitively state that that's true. It definitely does."

Epilogue

THE CLOCK SAID 11:07 P.M., and Edie told herself she was fine. Yes, they were supposed to have gone to see a show tonight, yes, Tyler was in surgery, yes, this was their first week together in her apartment, but still...

Her first instinct was to go to the diner, or call Barnaby and pick up a shift in his cab, but then she told herself she was being silly.

She flipped through the papers on the desk, looking for something to read, when she saw the DVD. It was home-made, and with only one word on it: Edie.

She knew the handwriting. Doctor's scrawl, she thought with a goofy smile. Curious about the contents, she slid it into the DVD player and sat back to watch.

It was Tyler, sitting in front of his computer, with non-mussed hair and a perfect Windsor knot. The ties were growing on her. As a bonus, she'd discovered they were great fun in bed.

"I know I'm supposed to be there with you. I know you're sitting there home alone, and I didn't want you to get lonely, or think I take you for granted. I made this, and I'm assuming that you're watching it, honestly, this feels very strange. No, that's not the point. I wanted to prove to you that I am no longer a brick. Actually, maybe I am, but I'm your brick. Please know that.

"I saw a woman on the street today, well, not today when you're watching this today, but today the day I made it today, and she didn't remind me of you. I know, because when I saw her, I wanted her to remind me of you. No, actually I wanted her to be you. And then I saw another woman with blond hair, she even had a streak, but she wasn't you, either. And then I knew that I would never see a woman who would remind me of you because you're the only you there is. On this planet. In my heart."

Into the camera he stared with those steady, serious eyes, and Edie pulled at the box of tissues, drying her tears, but they kept rolling down her cheeks. Fat, happy tears.

And the dark wasn't quite so lonely.

"I could sit here and talk about my feelings for another eight hours, but honestly, it would be about three more seconds of talk and another seven hours of awkward silence because I don't know what to say, at some level, I have not changed that much. Not yet. But I knew you liked mummies, so I checked out a book."

He cracked the spine and began to read:

"Around 3000 BC, the first Pharaohs ruled ancient Egypt—" then he looked up "—but you already knew that, because you know, you're smart that way."

After that, Edie pulled out her phone and sent him a text message.

Wake me when you get in. I love you. Edie.

After that, she picked up the phone and called the one person that she knew would be at home, the one person on the planet that she knew would understand.

"Hello, Mom. What are you doing?"

* * * * *

Harlequin Blaze

COMING NEXT MONTH

Available May 31, 2011

#615 REAL MEN WEAR PLAID!
Encounters
Rhonda Nelson

#616 TERMS OF SURRENDER
Uniformly Hot!
Leslie Kelly

#617 RECKLESS PLEASURES
The Pleasure Seekers
Tori Carrington

#618 SHOULD'VE BEEN A COWBOY
Sons of Chance
Vicki Lewis Thompson

#619 HOT TO THE TOUCH
Checking E-Males
Isabel Sharpe

#620 MINE UNTIL MORNING
24 Hours: Blackout
Samantha Hunter

You can find more information on upcoming
Harlequin® titles, free excerpts and more at
www.HarlequinInsideRomance.com.

REQUEST YOUR FREE BOOKS!
2 FREE NOVELS PLUS 2 FREE GIFTS!

Harlequin® Blaze™

red-hot reads!

YES! Please send me 2 FREE Harlequin® Blaze® novels and my 2 FREE gifts (gifts are worth about $10). After receiving them, if I don't wish to receive any more books, I can return the shipping statement marked "cancel." If I don't cancel, I will receive 6 brand-new novels every month and be billed just $4.24 per book in the U.S. or $4.71 per book in Canada. That's a saving of at least 15% off the cover price. It's quite a bargain. Shipping and handling is just 50¢ per book in the U.S. and 75¢ per book in Canada.* I understand that accepting the 2 free books and gifts places me under no obligation to buy anything. I can always return a shipment and cancel at any time. Even if I never buy another book, the two free books and gifts are mine to keep forever.

151/351 HDN FC4T

Name _____ (PLEASE PRINT) _____

Address _____ Apt. #

City _____ State/Prov. _____ Zip/Postal Code

Signature (if under 18, a parent or guardian must sign)

Mail to the **Reader Service:**
IN U.S.A.: P.O. Box 1867, Buffalo, NY 14240-1867
IN CANADA: P.O. Box 609, Fort Erie, Ontario L2A 5X3

Not valid for current subscribers to Harlequin Blaze books.

Want to try two free books from another line?
Call 1-800-873-8635 or visit www.ReaderService.com.

* Terms and prices subject to change without notice. Prices do not include applicable taxes. Sales tax applicable in N.Y. Canadian residents will be charged applicable taxes. Offer not valid in Quebec. This offer is limited to one order per household. All orders subject to credit approval. Credit or debit balances in a customer's account(s) may be offset by any other outstanding balance owed by or to the customer. Please allow 4 to 6 weeks for delivery. Offer available while quantities last.

Your Privacy—The Reader Service is committed to protecting your privacy. Our Privacy Policy is available online at www.ReaderService.com or upon request from the Reader Service.

We make a portion of our mailing list available to reputable third parties that offer products we believe may interest you. If you prefer that we not exchange your name with third parties, or if you wish to clarify or modify your communication preferences, please visit us at www.ReaderService.com/consumerchoice or write to us at Reader Service Preference Service, P.O. Box 9062, Buffalo, NY 14269. Include your complete name and address.

HBI I

Harlequin® Blaze™ brings you
New York Times *and* USA TODAY *bestselling author*
Vicki Lewis Thompson with three new steamy titles
from the bestselling miniseries SONS OF CHANCE

Chance isn't just the last name of these rugged
Wyoming cowboys—it's their motto, too!

Read on for a sneak peek at the first title,
SHOULD'VE BEEN A COWBOY

Available June 2011 only from Harlequin® Blaze™.

"THANKS FOR NOT TURNING ON THE LIGHTS," Tyler said. "I'm a mess."

"Not in my book." Even in low light, Alex had a good view of her yellow shirt plastered to her body. It was all he could do not to reach for her, mud and all. But the next move needed to be hers, not his.

She slicked her wet hair back and squeezed some water out of the ends as she glanced upward. "I like the sound of the rain on a tin roof."

"Me, too."

She met his gaze briefly and looked away. "Where's the sink?"

"At the far end, beyond the last stall."

Tyler's running shoes squished as she walked down the aisle between the rows of stalls. She glanced sideways at Alex. "So how much of a cowboy are you these days? Do you ride the range and stuff?"

"I ride." He liked being able to say that. "Why?"

"Just wondered. Last summer, you were still a city boy. You even told me you weren't the cowboy type, but you're…different now."

He wasn't sure if that was a good thing or a bad thing. Maybe she preferred city boys to cowboys. "How am I different?"

"Well, you dress differently, and your hair's a little longer. Your face seems a little more chiseled, but maybe that's because of your hair. Also, there's something else, something harder to define, an attitude…"

"Are you saying I have an attitude?"

"Not in a bad way. It's more like a quiet confidence."

He was flattered, but still he had to laugh. "I just admitted a while ago that I have all kinds of doubts about this event tomorrow. That doesn't seem like quiet confidence to me."

"This isn't about your job, it's about…your…" She took a deep breath. "It's about your sex appeal, okay? I have no business talking about it, because it will only make me want to do things I shouldn't do." She started toward the end of the barn. "Now, where's that sink? We need to get cleaned up and go back to the house. Dinner is probably ready, and I—"

He spun her around and pulled her into his arms, mud and all. "Let's do those things." Then he kissed her, knowing that she would kiss him back, knowing that this time he would take that kiss where he wanted it to go. And she would let him.

Follow Tyler and Alex's wild adventures in
SHOULD'VE BEEN A COWBOY
Available June 2011 only from Harlequin® Blaze™
wherever books are sold.

Copyright © 2011 by Vicki Lewis Thompson

Harlequin® *Blaze*™
red-hot reads

Do you need a cowboy fix?

NEW YORK TIMES BESTSELLING AUTHOR
Vicki Lewis Thompson

RETURNS WITH HER SIZZLING TRILOGY...

Sons of Chance

Chance isn't just the last name of these rugged Wyoming cowboys—it's their motto, too!

Take a chance...on a Chance!

Saddle up with:
SHOULD'VE BEEN A COWBOY (June)
COWBOY UP (July)
COWBOYS LIKE US (August)

**Available from Harlequin® Blaze™
wherever books are sold.**

www.eHarlequin.com

HB79622

Harlequin *Presents*

brings you

USA TODAY *bestselling author*

Lucy Monroe

with her new installment
in the much-loved miniseries

Royal Brides

Proud, passionate rulers—
marriage is by royal decree!

Meet Zahir and Asad—two powerful, brooding sheikhs
and masters of all they survey. They need brides,
and marriage in their kingdoms is by royal decree!

Capture a slice of royal life in this enthralling sheikh saga!

Coming in June 2011:
FOR DUTY'S SAKE

Available wherever
Harlequin Presents® books are sold.

www.eHarlequin.com

HP12993